SALT THE WATER

by Candice Iloh

DUTTON BOOKS

DUTTON BOOKS

An imprint of Penguin Random House LLC, New York

First published in the United States of America by Dutton Books,
an imprint of Penguin Random House LLC, 2023

Visit us online at PenguinRandomHouse.com.

Library of Congress Cataloging-in-Publication Data is available.

Printed in the United States of America

ISBN 9780593529317

1st Printing

LSCH
Design by Anna Booth
Text set in Minion Pro

for Sir, Nze Daniel Ibe Iloh

even from the ancestor realm your words and presence
still remind me that i always can make my own choice

"Don't be afraid to disappear—from it, from us—for a while,
and see what comes to you in the silence."
—Michaela Coel

"I'll

be loved

when no one's around."

—Smino

Dear Reader,

I always had this belief that I would never get to experience life past sixteen. Like many of us, I had been told a story of how it would end for me—for all of us—for so long that I couldn't conceive of me having much choice. Much say about my own future.

I imagined everything predetermined like a menu at a restaurant I couldn't even afford. My dreams came with caveats and clauses that I burdened myself with because I believed everyone's stories about me but my own. I learned to mimic and anticipate the needs of people around me in order to ensure that I would be loved. I learned how to be attractive. Become acceptable. Go along. I grew to be mutable and accepting of people's expectations of me in order to keep myself safe.

Because, again, I believed it was never in my hands anyway, and it was me that was wrong, not the world. Not the systems. Not the institutions. I wrote this story of Cerulean Gene for us whom Audre Lorde called those "who live at the shoreline / standing upon the constant edges of decision / crucial and alone . . . For all of us / this instant and this triumph / We were never meant to survive."

Dear Reader,

What if you live long?

What if *we* get to live long?

What if we do something different than *just* survive?

This story doesn't end how you think. I hope something here inspires you to consider other ways when the ones we've been given aren't working. I hope you're inspired to live beyond fear.

With Love,
Candice Iloh

SALT THE WATER

the problem with Mr. Schlauss

is that he ain't got lips
so he stays mad at us
for what the universe wouldn't give him
in a classroom full of

plump-lipped kids who always have
something smart to say
       that's what the principal keeps
       calling it during our visits: *smart*
       like it's some type of surprise or insult

when i thought
that's what everybody says
this place is for

school is me doing the same thing every day

sitting face forward
at a gum-crusted desk
that's covered in penis sketches
in a packed class

staring down the dry throat
of a person who's been given
the right to tell me
what to do cause they went to college

stuck under the spell of
chalkboard screams or
a promethean board light or
dry-erase marker fumes

until the bell rings to interrupt
it all again
for the next
study in adulthood

i can tell

he's not surviving his adulthood too well
i've never seen him without his morning Diet Coke
can smell the stale tinge of tobacco on his breath
even though i keep my distance

Mr. Schlauss takes another gulp
of the black stuff now caked into his teeth
releases a miserable sigh
says the same thing he's been repeating   for the last week

these tests are a game of decision-making
you don't really have to be smart to pass
all you've got to do is know how to answer
the questions   how to follow   the rules

all you've got to have
is common sense
we've been going over this

study the instructions   & you'll be fine

i study his face wondering

if this is what he thought he'd be doing with his life in his early twenties
his unironed T.J. Maxx button up half tucked into his too-long khakis
his dusty blond shag a hopeful cover-up to the patchy stubble washing
over his blotchy puffed face

Iya taught me that a swollen face is a sign somebody drinks too much
    beer
drinks so much the alcohol don't even move past your neck anymore
it just sits there for everybody to know what you spend most of your
    time doing
trying to cope

with the fact that you're stuck teaching in the Bronx postpandemic
when it really isn't postpandemic but the teacher shortage
is so bad your bare minimum gets overlooked
while you stay flying under the radar

doing more harm than good

he gulps & goes on some more about

process of elimination
cause & effect
main idea
critical lens

my eyes scan
the prep packet
ingesting words like
knack

hoopla
burgeoning
valid interpretation
appropriate literary elements

Mr. Schlauss's words
become a lowered hum
in my mind's movie score
as it starts bursting questions

thoughts like how
don't nobody i know
use these words & how
i wonder who decides what is   *valid*   *appropriate*

my desk jerks from the side

Zaria motions to the space under me
as usual there lies a crumpled piece of paper
full of analog text waiting for me to unravel

since this year the school's got a new system
locking up our phones in fabric pouches
that we can't open til we leave

i reach for it like clockwork
with my eyes focused on her legs
the only person i know who wears

fishnets & patent leather combat boots year-round
uncrinkling a note without looking away from her thighs
is our everyday romance

you really into this shit? lol

i let my smirk answer her question

pushing the note under the test prep packet
as Schlauss's dry monotone lecture comes back
into focus & reminds us how much of this test
makes up our total grade
& how much college acceptance
rides on our grades
& how college acceptance
determines the direction of our lives

indicate whether you agree or disagree
with the statement as you have interpreted it
choose two works you have read
that you believe best support your opinion

use specific references
to appropriate literary elements
to develop
your analysis

tell them what they
want to hear to prove
you've got some sense
to prove

you can achieveachieveachieve   success

my hand shoots up without thinking to stop myself

& Mr. Schlauss rolls his eyes
letting out another miserable sigh
before stopping in the middle
of his instructions

       yes . . . what is it, Sara—

—*it's Cerulean.*

       yes, sure, Ms. Gene
       what is it now?

—*it's CERULEAN*   *& i was wondering*
What they mean by "appropriate"—

      Cerulean Gene   *we don't have time*
      for this today, i'm sure you know
      what "appropriate" means

—*yes, i know the definition, but that's why i'm asking*
we never read the kind of books we like in here
so how will we know if our examples from the references are

appropriate?

who decides whose interpretation   *is right?*
maybe you
should   *specify?*

he laughs to himself

as if to say:
if i don't know what the test
means by
appropriate
how is it that i know
what it means
to *specify?*

Cerulean i don't need to specify

anything here
you need to be paying
closer attention
to what we read
& what i say
in this class
& if you're too busy reading
The Hate U Give
to pay enough
attention to
an actual
great American classic
like, say, Huck Finn
maybe
you should get your
priorities
straight

Iya taught me

that it's good
to take deep breaths
or walks
or to drink water to make sure
i've taken time
before i speak out in anger
that way i'm clear when i finally
say what i gotta say
so i take the hall pass
to do all three

outside the classroom
with the door closed
behind me
Mr. Schlauss's squeaky voice
becomes an even more
distant hum
in the empty hallway

i walk, counting the tiles
taking in the ugly burgundies, yellows
& creams—a color scheme that i've been
staring at within these walls
for the past three years now

thinking about
what it means
for my priorities
to be straight

after a few laps around

the junior class floor
i pause standing
in front of the GSA office

       a club the school was probably mandated to have
think more
about Mr. Schlauss's suggestion
that i be anything that i am not
straight
uniform
binary
that there is only his right
& our wrong
how i should
read something
he deems *real*   or fail

i stare at the out-of-date GSA poster

for five more minutes
call it a guided meditation
for queer Black kids who considered
snapping on their problematic white teacher
when the rainbow wasn't enough

next to the poster & rainbow-lined door

stretch large windows
a darkened chemistry lab
housed on the other side
that ain't been used in years

never seeing anybody
go in or out between classes
everybody's been convinced
it must be the scene of a crime

that nobody thinks is worth
cleaning up so we the phone-deprived
use these windows like mirrors
to see ourselves in its reflection

trying to avoid spending
too much time in rarely cleaned
bathrooms reserved for students
i stare at myself taking in another breath

then exhale thinking about Iya
& how i'll tell her all about this tonight
pull my locs into a knot
to give my neck some air

take another deep breath
& go
back

good to see you back with a new hairstyle

Mr. Schlauss curves me
as i return the pass
just in time for the bell to ring
signaling that we're now allowed
to leave for lunch

hang out for a bit Cerulean

Zaria grazes the hairs of my forearm
gently reminding me to meet her outside
at our spot after i find out
whatever Mr. Schlauss's problem is

i hold her scent waiting for the class to clear

i just wanted to remind you

> *—Mr. Schla—*

—no no no no no
i'm talking now
you're in my class
& these are my rules
& the next time
you want to leave my classroom
you need to ask me first
you can't just go around
doing whatever it is
that you want

i had to use the bathroom

a lie pressed through my clenched teeth
but that don't matter

i need to ask
for permission to piss?

    Cerulean
    the next time you need

    to urinate?
    you need to raise your hand

    & if it's at
    the appropriate time   he pauses, feeling himself

    i might let you go   he says

his back already turning to me

there's no point

in me talking to the back of Mr. Schlauss's head
when he's already made up his mind about me
but i still stand there steps behind him staring into
the sad crease of his freckled neck smiling into it
Iya says we should smile at our enemies   smile
that we got joy even when it's clear they struggling

i pull in air & let it out slowly, quiet looking at
his trashed desk piled with old papers i doubt
he actually reads   test packets & textbooks
older than both my parents' ages combined   wonder
why he believes in any of this stuff when it seems
like he ain't believe in himself enough to do
something he actually cares about for money

his Teach for America manual so faithfully kept
at the corner of his desk to remind him
he's only got to survive one more year teaching
inner-city youth   one more year of service
so the government can pay him back everything
he's losing as he works

to become a master

Zaria has mastered the art

of seducing me out of my midday misery

now far away from arbitrary school rules
& Schlauss's orders i exhale
then press my lips against hers
standing below the Pop Smoke mural
freshly painted on the side of the corner deli
just one block down from school
she takes my hand

what that stuffy white boy want this time

our check-ins always full with questions
to each other about how we're surviving
failed corporate executives turned teachers
who were once paid more to work in an office
i kiss her hand & shrug

he wanted me to raise my hand next time i need to pee

we laugh at the idea

& she pulls the jingling door to the bodega open for me / the smell
of bacon egg & cheese / up our noses walking to the back where she /
orders her tuna melt / my falafel wrap / her arm curved tight around
my waist / it still feels like summer even though October creeps up
on us / like lonely uncles catcalling from lawn chairs outside project
housing at all hours of the day / i reach for my wallet to pay just before
Zaria stops me / *i got you babe*

hands hover methodically above the blazing grills

that so many things have touched

while the cooks' eyes
bounce back & forth between
this surge of lunch orders &
two obnoxiously large tv screens
mounted above chopped cheese
overstuffed deli sandwiches
& buttered toasting rolls

a dramatic voice-over actor
gives us all the backstory of Christina Wright
youngest known contestant of *Dystopia Tank Race*
an outlaw among a cast of old heads who
think she's too idealistic finding
her motives for being on the show to be

'cute'

for Christina Wright, the stakes are high
& the tension is even higher!
while veteran contestants play the game to
plot and scheme for the American dream
Christina says her dream includes
a different America!
& the camera pans

to a sentimental montage of how hard
Christina had it growing up

how hard Christina has worked
in her communities
how hard Christina seemed
to work every day of her life
for a future the other contestants

have never even had to imagine

Zaria lifts herself up

onto her tiptoes to hand
Mike the bodega guy her cash
across the too-high counter
that used to be split by plexiglass
& stocked with hand sanitizer
now returned to open air
jars of soft mints
Twix Minis
incense
knockoff phone chargers

drops back down to her heels
waiting for the change
while grazing her platinum buzz cut
the way she always does
when she's hungry
anxious to go
Mike hands her back the change
clinging seconds too long
suddenly offended by her
snatching her hand back
in disgust

be nice, baby
i'm good guy
why you being
so mean today

today we're caught

in the lunch crowd we usually dodge
beating everybody else to the spot
most of us upperclassmen go to now
that we got open lunch & can go
anywhere we want as long
as we're back before the sixth-period bell

usually Mike doesn't try shit with either of us
feeling bold enough to squeeze a hand
that doesn't want his attention   my eyes unglue
from the television and i push up
to the counter ready to tell him to fuck off
but Zaria beats me to it   her voice so quick   piercing

that the incoming crowd parts as we leave

most days

we get back in time enough
for us to eat & find Irvin selling
snacks he's got stocked in his locker
Blow Pops   Takis   whatever else
gullible underclassmen want
to make it through to ninth period
& back to life beyond these walls

but this time not finding
the usual crowd flooded
around his locker
we know we'll be eating lunch
outside

we see red vapor floating

from behind the back walls of the school
& find Irvin & Jai hovered over Jai's
Creation of the Week
Zaria coughs to announce our presence
i wave fumes, slapping hands with each
of my best friends

awww shit! we got an audience!
you sure you ready for the world
to see this, sib? Irv asks Jai
i don't know, it might be too early
you know we can't rush beauty

Jai lifts their head revealing
a bandana tied tight across
nose & mouth & sits back
on their heels capping the spray can
to then rest their hands on their knees

i guess we can let these inner city youth
get a lil sneak peek   you know we
always gotta give back to the community
& they cuttin art programs left & right
go on and let these poor kids get a closer look

Zaria rolls her eyes

at Irv & Jai's daily
art dealer & artist
role-play

pulls Irv into a hug
like she hadn't
seen him in weeks

though this
is a version of our scene
almost every day

you just did all this
today? i ask Jai,
impressed

yeah, sib
Ms. Lorna walked into class
basically in clown drag

she already be lookin
mad crazy & the fact
that she tried to cover it up with that mess?

i was inspired

i call this one
"Goddess Doth Not Like Ugly"
you like?

the three of us bust out laughing

til we realize Jai is serious
never having been good at naming their work

removing their bandana now completely
Jai reveals a freshly bleached mustache & goatee

to match their eyebrows, vibe & mood
their new look for this week only

y'all laughin now but don't come askin me
for nothin when i sell this baby on fifth ave

they right though, that's where all the rich types be
Zaria chimes in, in support of our tender friend

could probably get a solid rack for this
i ain't laugh that hard, Jai   don't forget about me

yo, i got five hundred once selling a piece over there
Jai starts, eyes glazing over looking out at nothing

Ms. Lorna always talkin about fine art this & that
but them rich folks love them some street graffiti

we all stop talking for a second like we
were all thinking the same thing

but for real though, Irv says breaking the silence
how much all y'all got so far? for our plan

how we doin on money?

last summer we'd come up with The Pact: realizing P.S. 5000 would never send us somewhere worth the trip we'd pool our money to book tickets to sunny California for a summer / we always been just a bunch of Bronx babies knowing nothing much but bodegas, superspreader house parties & subway horror stories / but we knew something else might be on the other side / we all knew we needed to find something different than the go-to-college or bad-reality-show conveyor belt so our hustle became dreaming about what it might be like to live a different life / one filled with art / love / sunshine on our faces / not all of us were artists but we knew we wanted to create some other kind of world / somewhere / that'd allow all of us to be ourselves / something like the world Iya & Baba had made for my brother & me

but something we'd never seen

a thick spicy gust

of Baba's famous salmon curry surrounds
Zaria & me the minute i push open
my front door & lead her in

the whole house smells heavy
of ginger, garlic, cumin, onion
& whatever else he be puttin

in his favorite cast-iron skillet
every time he's off & home able to
cook for like the millionth time in his week

Zaria's been here enough times
to beat me to the shoes-off-
before-anything-else rule

& is guided into the kitchen
to hug my dad
before i can even get to him

but i don't even have to be back there
to know the kitchen counter
is covered in every pot & every vegetable

we own

we own this little piece of world

is how Baba & Iya once explained our house
to me & Airyn back when we moved
to the South Bronx & i was still
in the eighth grade
Airyn being three at the time probably
ain't know what they was talkin about
but i liked the sound of it

ours

Baba said *this little brownstone*
we got here is for us to do
what we want   live
how we want without landlords
tellin us how to be
Iya said *we gon' build us*
a good life here

no matter what's going on outside

i pass through the kitchen to meet Airyn outside

Zaria & Baba talk like old friends
barely looking my way as i jog
back down the stairs & behind them

i find Airyn hovering over sunflowers
daisies, & lavender Iya helped him
plant before summer started as his
end-of-the-year fourth-grade school project

his nose & hands graze each of his
creations as if he's seeing them
for the first time & like they're
the coolest things he's ever witnessed

he's so into his plant babies that he
barely notices when i appear directly behind him
hearing me clear my throat yanks him
out of the world he creates in our backyard

yo don't be walkin up on me like that

or what? you'll bash me with the head
of one of your big, tall sunflowers?

maybe slice me with the sharp leaves
of your prickly lavender?

finally taking his eyes off his plants
he rolls them at me

i'd telepathically make you trip over
something you couldn't even see

you'd be coming down the stairs
not even worried about nothin

then bam!   you'd fall face-forward
as if your foot got jammed

on an invisible log
you'd be so confused

—confused like you are about what
the word telepathically actually means?

he shrugs looking back at his flower bed
like he doesn't have energy to waste on me

you know what i mean
i'd get you with my mind

for always messin with me
you wouldn't even know what hit you

—i know you wouldn't actually
hurt nobody, Airyn, come on

you know i ain't mean to scare you
he looks back up at me, his face softening

say something so i know you behind me
before you come down the stairs, okay?

i got you

won't happen again i tell him
kneeling down beside him to get
a closer look at what he's so into

it feels like at least five minutes
pass before Airyn says anything to me
while we sit there staring into dirt

what are we gon' do when it gets
too cold for them to stay alive
the question surprises me but i answer

without thinking

we find a new place to keep them
so they can   *we got lots of space in the house*
i'm sure Iya & Baba will let you bring them in

the answer i thought would help doesn't

but the sunflowers won't survive inside there
they're supposed to get a lot of light & air
they can't get it anywhere when it's winter

he's right

well then it means we gotta say goodbye
until next time   *they'll go away for a little while but*
then they'll come back next year

as new sunflowers ready to live a different life
maybe think of it like hibernation the same way
the bears be goin into their caves until it's safe

to come back

you keep sayin come back

like what you mean ain't that they're gonna die
i'm old enough to know they just gonna die, Cerulean

—not true, Bubby, the name only i call him
i learned about plants & shit, too, you know

they're not that different from the stuff i'm tryna grow
i remind him gesturing to my small garden plot across the yard

i didn't go to no fancy school like you do now
but i read books & i know something

who you think Iya sent to the store to buy
all this outdoor stuff for your project last year?

old man in the plant shop rapped me up so long
i knew everything i needed to know to start something of my own

i wasn't lying to you, Bubby
somehow   when it gets real cold outside

these things shrivel up & look like they dead
but their seeds go back into the soil

& when it's spring again
those same seeds bring it back to life

i leave you outside with your brother

for ten minutes & you already
out here talkin about reincarnation

can you let my son stare
at flower petals in peace?

both Airyn & i look
up the back door stairs

just now noticing Zaria & Baba
been eavesdropping this whole time

he got home from school hours ago
why don't you let the child play

—ain't that all they do at his school
all day, anyway? i ask (serious question)

& don't they encourage him to, like
learn from everything, hands-on? come on, Baba

i'm just teaching Airyn about life the way i see it
i'm a good person to learn from, too i assure him

winking

Baba winks back at me

mocking another one of my rants about Airyn's school situation
knowing i'll never shut up about the fact
that he gets to go to an Afrocentric Montessori school
while i've been stuck in the public school system

pretty much my whole life so far

how he gets to learn about farming & art & community
from real-life situations & teachers who let them
explore & make mistakes & talk back
when something don't make sense to them

while i'm stuck in stiff-ass classrooms
facing the same direction every day
staring down out-of-touch white men
who don't care if i really learn

who measure what i know by how well i do on a test

at this point Airyn's tuned us all out

& puts a hand back on the soil
as if testing to see if it's ready for water
while i drop my case & sniff the air hoping
Baba's meal is almost ready for my belly

he signals me to come back in
& leave Airyn alone again to do his thing
so i dust off my knees & meet Zaria
back at the top of the steps

as Baba leads us both to the kitchen counter

in one corner of the kitchen counter

is a spread of
sliced plantain
chopped beets
& black rice
soaking
in a bowl of water

next to it Baba's set out
coconut oil
olive oil
pink salt
paprika
minced garlic

at the stove i see
steam rising
from the
cast-iron skillet
where he's
already

finished
the curry
now waiting
for us
to help
with side dishes

Baba pushes the plantain & the beets

in front of Zaria & me & stares back
have you washed your hands?

says, *y'all already know what to do*
turns back toward a boiling pot

to add the rice
& salt the water

i go to wash my hands while Zaria grabs the salt

i stand over the sink
watching the water splash
over the soap suds i'd lathered
all the way up to my elbows
the exact way
Baba asks we do it

i walk back over to the counter
sit with my hands up
hovering midair as if i'm entering
surgery & need to avoid
contamination before touching
the patient on the operating table

Baba grabs me my tools
black pepper
minced garlic
olive oil
shakes the pepper
over the beets first

then adds globs
of the garlic
douses the whole thing
with the oil last
offers gloves   i refuse as always
& he tells me   to go head

of chopped beets that i've grown myself / i mix the seasonings in / both my hands becoming bloodied / with the bright magenta juice / a deep pink stain / that'll probably take days / to fully wash out / & Baba gives me this job / cause he knows i love / getting lost in the pigment of my own creation / & the aroma / as the mixture of its scent rises / so lost / that my shoulders drop / my breath slows / & i'm ready to talk / about pretty much / anything / even school

so Zaria was tellin me about how school went today

you wanna   elaborate?
i roll my eyes & keep squishing

Baba is patient
all about the long game

bread for this dinner began
before breakfast

when he scooped a portion
of his funky sourdough starter

his "mother" as he calls it
into a bowl with waterfloursaltsugar

twelve hours later that mess
is now four long smooth rolls
on a board before him

Baba aligns them
begins to braid them like hair
good one, Baba   i bet
Mr. Schlauss gon' make sure

we know that one for the test
he laughs already understanding the joke

i look over at Zaria wondering how much
she's told him & how much he needs

to be caught up
out the corner of my eye

his hands move so quick
neither of us notice the loaf disappear

into the oven

Zaria shrugs her shoulders

goes to rinse the rice water
over the sink while i focus
all my energy into the sound
of my beets squishing
between my fingers
my hands becoming
heavily coated
in oily seasoning

feel Baba still leaned in
waiting for me to quit
stalling & spill the goods

i just don't understand the point
of spending every day
learning stuff we'll never
really use
just to take a test
from some stiff-ass white dude
who just likes
tellin us what to do

mocking my loose
choice of words
in front of Baba

AHAHAHAHA!
STIFF-ASS!
AHAHAHAHA!

Baba walks over
cracks the door
gives him a look

tells him
oh, that's funny, right?
chill with all that

we know your sib
gets a little passionate
when they're tryna

express themself
but don't you go repeating that
at school

even though i couldn't see Airyn's face

i know the shady smirk
he   gave Baba knowing
he wouldn't get in trouble
for using a curse word
out of context
as long as he ain't
call somebody
an asshole
or tell some kid
he'd beat their ass
or tell his teacher
to kiss his Black ass
there's no real consequence
for him saying a phrase
he overheard
at home
with no intent
to disrespect

no disrespect Baba

but that's really all i'm in the mood
to say about it right now
i rather us just cook
instead of talk
about this

talk about what

are Iya's first words
as she saunters into the kitchen
mixing the curry aroma
with her chlorine-soaked BO

she makes her way
around the kitchen island
to wrap her arms around
Baba's waist before

mushing her face
into the nape of his neck
then lifting it to smile across
the counter at us

really i just wanted
her to be home before
i went off about school stuff
once again

not wanting
to have to repeat
my complaints to her
after spilling my guts

to Baba

Baba turns to face Iya

clutches the small
of her back with his left hand
leans against her
& reaches around
her to turn off the stove
with his right

in between kisses
he changes the subject briefly
damn, baby
i feel like i done jumped
in a swimming pool

the showers stopped
working over at the center?
Iya kisses him back him
saying she skipped that step
not wanting to miss his famous curry
ain't you happy i made it
home?

home is always

filled with random food aromas
or the smell
of chlorine, sweat
an amber body oil
my mama's scent
but rarely clashing together
all at the same time

with Baba working long hours
at the restaurant
we're always tryna find the time
to be together somehow
mushing up
all our individual stuff

my parents never
stopped living their lives
when they had us
they just moved things around
so that all of us could have whatever
we needed to keep becoming

ourselves

Zaria & i move ourselves

away from the counter where Iya & Baba
whisper secret love nothings to each other
under their breath & forget us sitting there

Zaria pulls the glass baking pan
closer to us as i lift my hands
out of the beet bowl & away to the sink

she pours the pieces out & i
meet her at the preheated oven
after cleaning the last bits of minced garlic

from between my fingers
the heat rushes out at our faces
opening its door

she glides
my favorite side dish in   says
i ain't know you wasn't ready

i ain't mean
to put you on the spot like that
with Baba

Baba been cooking since before both me & Airyn was born & i heard he went through hella shit to get where he is. Used to tell me all the time how kitchen boys would haze him for wanting to be the best. Would tell him he ain't gon' do nothin but make pizzas in Brooklyn the rest of his life like everybody else. That he should keep all that fancy cooking to himself & stick to the recipe.

The recipe to get me to talk usually was simple: Baba cooks. Iya is home. Zaria is chillin next to me with her hand resting on my thigh or smoothing down my arm hair. i used to tell her she was weird for that til she called me out about the fact that i like it. Zaria's hand glides down my arm & into my right hand. She squeezes it. Another part of the recipe.

i take a breath

while everybody lifts heaps
of salmon   beets   rice
into their mouths
leaned over a wooden table at the center
of our backyard

even though ain't nothing
scary about talking to Iya & Baba
it still takes me time to shake off
the poison they try to inject
me with at school

that's what that place wants:
to get in my blood, take my brain

tryna make me think
what i have to say is just
a dumb kid's opinion   just
me being aggy about
having to do
what all kids gotta do

but in our backyard while we eat together
i know my parents won't trip   i know
they'll listen without interrupting to tell me
that how i reacted to Mr. Schlauss
was *inappropriate*   *rude*

they won't just side with the adult acting like
only adults have the authority in every situation   nah
at the end of the day Iya & Baba are with me
no matter what happened

they won't
make me feel like
i was wrong
for pushing
back

so when i got back

from the bathroom
he tells me i need to
ask permission

tells me i can't
just do whatever i want
to do

when i question having
to ask permission
to take care of myself

he says it's his classroom
that the next time
i gotta go

i gotta
ask first

then he'll decide

if
the timing
is appropriate

Iya & Baba's shoulders touch

like people who don't never get sick of each other
their eyes never leave my face as i feel

my arms flail around me telling more of another story
where me & Mr. Schlauss face off in a game of

who will give in to the other first   but they listen like
it's the best movie they've ever seen & they

can't risk missing a moment by looking away
if Zaria didn't love eating with her hands

one of hers would be resting heavily on my thigh
while i went on about these tests that Airyn don't never

have to worry about at his school where he
gets treated like a person who has choices

the night breeze shakes the maple tree above us
then grazes my face like a hand as i get tired

of talking even though nobody here minds listening
except for maybe Airyn   i pause & look over at him

catch him fishing   shiitake mushrooms
from the curry, carefully separating the pile

from what he wants to eat & inching
the unwanted fungi toward me

Iya swallows another piece of bread
then lifts her half-filled mason jar

from the table, gesturing toward
the rest of us to do the same

Cheers to Cerulean surviving another day ina dis blasted Babylon system

Iya always leads with a joke

not because she doesn't take me seriously
but because she says she refuses to raise
somebody so consumed by what's messed up
in the world that they don't never get to laugh

we all laugh at Iya's silly rasta impersonations

comparing me to the long-locked dudes
selling oils, shea butter & handmade soaps
        along the sidewalks dressed
in old-school Biggie T-shirts with their natural
hair pulled up into their loc socks

it started when i stopped combing my hair

Baba said he liked how my look screamed
that i was my own person
while Iya overused the word *bombaclot,*
asked me if i was done eating animals &
poked at me about what conspiracy theories

i'd developed about the news

but seriously Cerulean

you know this ain't new
we've talked about this
a million times

that place is a means
to an end   your ticket

up out of here someday

finishing this phase
of your life means
you can move on

they won't be able
to keep you here
unable to live your life

you can't let that man
sway you   every time
he tries to knock you

off center

Iya is always talkin about our center

the place where we feel balanced
& we're at peace with the world
no matter what's going on outside

where nothing can touch you cause you
know who you are   you are zen
above it all the noise & mess

unless   what's going on outside
is an everyday part of your life
to the point where the center seems

to be moving further & further away
tipped so far left that balance
is nearly impossible   to hold on to

it's impossible to move on in this story

without pointing out the fact
that Airyn
gets to go to a better school
than Zaria & i do
that Airyn
don't have to transcend
all the gaslighting
or the groupthink
that Airyn
ain't never been told
going to school
is just a means
to an end
that Airyn
always had a say
in what he was
made of
that Airyn
will always
have way less

to unlearn

at the end of the day

it all comes down to money

the big old fancy school
with all the resources & love
filled with teachers who care
costs a grip   something
Iya & Baba ain't have
when i first started out

Baba was just a sous chef
shadowing at other people's restaurants
Iya was working her way up
from after-school care worker
to lead swim instructor at the rec center
& it wasn't enough

to shell out thousands of dollars

when i could just deal with it
like all the other kids   just deal with
the overcrowded classrooms
the outdated textbooks   ancient libraries   unskilled teaching fellows
i could just deal with it

undo it all at home   so i can go to school   for free

oh, so y'all just over there playin house huh

over there
cookin dinner
& shit
Moms & Dad
cool with y'all
up in the room
together
unsupervised
y'all really
too grown
for me, sib

Irv & Jai
cheese into the screen
as Zaria & i
look back at them
her arms
draped over
my shoulders
hands dangling
in front
of my chest

she kisses
my right cheek
to give them
more reason
to talk shit

knowing they
both wish
they could
have somebody
in their rooms
without their parents
creepin on
them

clearly y'all some creeps

Starin all googly-eyed into the screen
on some real voyeur shit like we're
your favorite R-rated movie &
the only time y'all see anything
this beautiful is when y'all parents
gone somewhere & y'all sneak
to watch grown folks handlin
they business

Irv & Jai make it their business

to be a little more dramatic
to talk shit & hiss loudly
for a few more minutes
as Zaria plants a few more
soft kisses   into my forehead
my neck   my cheeks

then Zaria tells them we've got to go

Jai says goodbye but makes sly comments
about how they know we've got things to do
that they know we need to get back
to babymaking   or whatever it is teens who
get to do whatever they want in they parents' house
do in their free time

Zaria stares back into the screen
with a mischievous smile   one hand
on top of mine & reminds them
that can't nobody in this bedroom
make any babies

fact is
without adoption or doctors
us queers can't
make families without intention
without planning
without trying
without care

after we end the FaceTime i can tell Zaria is trying

not to press the issue of my behavior & our big plans
to get up out of here but she leans back on my bed
elbows behind her & says something anyway:

it ain't too much longer babe
i know Mr. Schlauss be doin a lot & all
but you can't keep letting him get to you like that

you know he'd just love to see your ass
get suspended   or worse
& we can't have that   we're way too close   to the finish line

she then reminds me of the goalposts   the pact
we made with the group   to save all our coins   & not
do anything that would land us in summer school   or worse

she sits back up & grazes the top of her head
waiting for me to respond & confirm that i understand
my eyes can't help but survey her legs

down to her feet preferring to focus there
instead of making promises that feel too hard to keep
instead of making promises that would silence me

so i lie

i tell her

that i know
that we are
counting down
only about six
more months
of sitting behind
old desks
attached
to seats that
no longer
& never did
fit us

that i won't
talk back
every time
Mr. Schlauss
makes me small
like i'm
at his mercy
or like
his word
against mine
meaning
i always
lose

that i will

keep
my head down
do the work
keep
my mouth shut
not disturb
whatever so-called
peace
comes from
compliance

we scorch under the Friday afternoon sun

each of us standing ten feet apart waiting
for Chanel to fill our empty hands with seeds

under our feet lies moist soil she says we can call our own
on these half days of each week that most kids skip / thinking

nobody will notice or care
        Zaria & i stay until the dismissal bell chimes feeling like

this is what we wish the whole day was made of:
today we fill dirt with babies that'll bear actual fruit we can eat

it isn't the first time i've ever done this but it is always
one of the few times anything in this school feels like it's mine

Zaria eyeballs me making sure i hang on to every word
says if i don't respect nothing else,

i could respect this

i respect Chanel cause she technically isn't a teacher

not like the others at least

she's what she calls a teaching artist:
someone the school pays less
than a regular teacher who comes
once a week to teach us things
i wish the rest of school would catch on to

like
how food grows from soil   water
the air its ingredients grow in
how to respect   the land

like
how to be excited about the earth
how to play & explore
how to wonder & discover

like
how to be a kid playing with sand
at a playground surrounded
by fire ants

that you're not afraid of
cause you know
ain't no insects worried about

somebody who hasn't come
to disrupt
their home

somebody who hasn't come
just to take
to capitalize

to knock their lives
down

there are no winners in this class

not in the way you might think, Chanel tells us
pacing the otherwise empty yard behind P.S. 5000

this class isn't about who can do it biggest
who can do it better   or survival of the fittest

this class isn't some gauntlet or race where the fastest
or most ruthless reaps the greatest reward

it is
about growth & creation when the rest
of the world teaches you how to destroy

it is
about your relationship to the soil & what
you've come to offer her in exchange for life

it is
about giving back to the very thing that you came from
*   about taking only, in exchange, what you need*

it is
about taking care of what the earth gives to us
in the face of corporate greed when so many

claim there isn't enough
for us all

all of us follow her with our eyes

as she weaves in & out
of the small plots we've been
given to experiment with
& she asks me
to remind the class

what's the first thing
we must remember
about planting seeds
& i come back to life
back to the soil i'm standing on

remember what she said last class
that growing things
    takes focus
    takes paying attention to the weather
    takes patience   protection   lots of love

    takes staying present
    takes ritual & routine
    takes experimentation
    takes time

our first Friday with Chanel Aioki

no one had to tell us it was her
walking down the hallway toward us
casually adorned under a hot pink beanie
large silver hoops   wide enough
to graze her shoulders   strong & pushed back
wearing an oversized graphic tee
with tie-dyed cargo jeans stuffed into white combat boots

her crossbody bag looked like it was trying
to be both birthday cake & balloons on one side of her body
while, on the other, she carried what she'd later
call her lesbian toolbox full of gardening equipment
a Bluetooth speaker with a jar of candy she told us
was necessary for proper learning   because *learning should be fun*

none of us knew what to think but we liked her

no one else in this school looks like her
or even talks like her for that matter   her presence
like a crash course in Japanese street fashion dropped in the middle
of a small, quiet Black town even though we're Bronx kids
in a big-ass city who claim there's nothing we haven't seen
that day my eyes trailed the bleach splatter
that decorated the bottom half of her small frame

the way she seemed to happily drown
under everything she wore   style
like the apocalypse & video game lore exploded on her

she introduced herself to me   to us
by her first name   promised to learn all of ours
punctuated everything with her hands
wrists loose & fingers dancing while she spoke
making it hard not to stare until she
pushed through our attitudes   our glares

that first day in her class as seniors
        with fewer classes & certified teachers
        wandering the halls
        than the day we left them not knowing
        when we came back from doing all
        from inside our apartment walls expecting
        a virus would end life as we knew it

that nothing & everything would be the same that first day Chanel
        invited us to follow her outside
        to find our space   on the yard

the yard is buzzing

with the sudden movement & clink
of small shovels & shoes pressing down
into the earth as Chanel walks around
to each of us allowing us to choose our seeds
we have a choice of herbs   plant flesh
or both   but there's a whole spread:

basil mint sage rosemary
cilantro thyme lavender
blueberry beans lemon
all kinds of greens like
chard spinach kale plus scallions
potatoes peppers cherry tomatoes

it all makes me want to flex
standing next to kids who'd never
done this before   me carrying more
experience under my belt than the average
public school kid but Chanel's words
echo in my head   that my skills   aren't what this is about

she lowers her box of seeds to the ground

between me & Zaria & calls us out
to come choose what we want to plant
Zaria eyes me   we've gone over this
we want to learn as many herbs as we can

first

mint for our periods   headaches   infection   sleep
lavender for daily stressors   Jai's asthma   Irv's eczema   all our acne
rosemary for when Zaria wants to roast us potatoes like she's learned
      from Baba
sage for my stomach problems   Zaria's depression   for clearing

energy

Chanel praises our choices calling us
wise & ahead of our time
we both flush under these affirmations
feeling capable under her gentle eye

after class in the cafeteria Jai has their textbooks

laid out across our entire table & their gaze
flies across all of them as if attempting somehow
to absorb all the information through telepathy

yo i can feel all of it going in   i've been practicing
if i do this   for at least   fifteen minutes every hour
*   for the rest of the day*
i'll be ready right before our first regents   tomorrow

Zaria slurps her chocolate milk
Irv stuffs more fries into his mouth than he should
i part my lips for the remainder of my fruit cup
Jai continues to laser beam down at the pages   unaware

of how ridiculous they sound

sounds like we all gon' be up tonight huh, Irv asks us

stay up for what?
to pretend
we've read
Catcher in the Rye
The Great Gatsby
or Macbeth
ain't no way
i'm doing that
i tell him
besides
Mr. Schlauss
said it
hisself:
the regents
ain't got nothin
to do with bein
smart
or whatever it
is they keep
calling kids
who read
whatever book
they give us
without ever
questioning
how little
we relate

yo forget being able to relate

we just tryna get up out of here
& this is our last year so
i feel you, babe
but we not gon' change
these teachers' minds
in six months

i hate when Zaria is right
& wrong at the same time
it's not that i want the teachers
to change their minds
it's just that in order to survive
this hellscape

i gotta quiet
mine

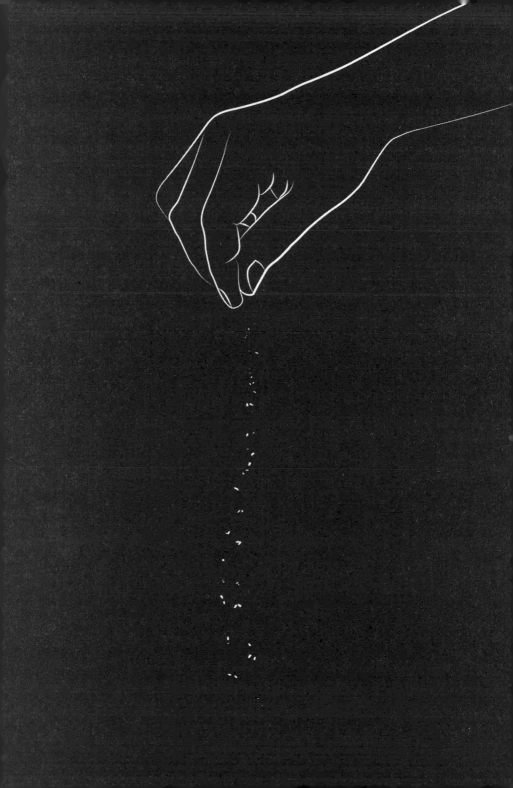

a lot of mornings in the Gene house

are something out of most kids' wildest dreams
somehow there are always options for breakfast
nag champa & palo santo burning
one or two bodies rested cross-legged
on Iya's blanket
together taking a second to breathe
facing a window
to chant
to find stillness
many of my classmates
never seen
in their whole lives

first
i wake Airyn
& Airyn wakes Iya
& sometimes
he joins her in
sansho
& sometimes it's me
chanting
Nam-Myōhō-Renge-Kyō
three times
after we speak
Baba's name
to hold space for him
already dressed in his kitchen
turning on lights checking

incoming deliveries
freezers
pantries
countertops
for what
the restaurant will need
for today's
service

there is no service at our subway stop

as always below ground i wait for the 1 train
glad no one can text or call me & i can't scroll the internet
where my anxiety skyrockets on mornings like this

my hands open & clench into fists
over & over in my jacket pockets trying
not to think too hard about facing Mr. Schlauss's ugly ass

Baba says an empty heart with no love in it or good intentions
makes a person ugly no matter what they look like
that everybody is inherently beautiful

until they open their mouths to expose
all the bitter

i stop in the corner deli

on the way in to P.S. 5000 to curb the bitter
rising in my throat   needing something sweet
after skipping breakfast this morning
believing it might come right back up   or worse:
taste like nothing amid the flips
of my belly's insides

i search below the counter for candy
disappointed to discover i'm here before
the shelves have been stocked for the day
nothing but boring sugar-free gummy bears
stale butter cookies & saltless crackers
the stuff nobody wants

i reach for the gummy bears
my best option & order a hot peppermint tea
over the counter
Baba would frown at this sad excuse
for a first meal of the day
but he'd still be proud

i remembered that the first thing
to go on the stomach in the morning
should be hot water
to calm the nerves   curb
an unsettled gut
help   push all the bad stuff   out

you know i could have hooked you up, son

now you out here eating diet candy   *struggling*
Irv scolds me as he closes his locker

he leans back on it, dropping his backpack
to the floor near his feet

what good would that have done, bro? i ask
would have been like stealing from ourselves

you supposed to be making as much money as possible
hookups & family discounts is bad for business

i mean you right & all but sugar-free gummy bears
is bad news, my guy, he says eyeballing the slowly disappearing pack

Jai slaps hands with him as they walk up overhearing us
& agrees: *yo my granny had a bowl of them shits*

on her coffee table last time i was over at her house or whatever
i took a handful cause a bitch was hungry, okay?

she was in the kitchen scooting around singing gospel songs
& i said whatever   *let me see what these gummies talkin about*

SIB   *it only took thirty minutes & i was ALL the way messed up*
i ain't even want no cobbler or nothin after that

was scared my butt couldn't hold anything in
the doctors gon' tell Granny to lay off the sugar

so now she's eating sugar-free this & carb-free that
but ain't say nothin about aspartame

now that's
the real poison

fam don't you think it's too early

to be talkin about bootyholes Zaria asks
both me & Irv dying
laughing at our friend's past misfortune
while squirming in disgust
thinking about what went down
after those thirty minutes
at the same time

yeah   i honestly rather not, i say
pulling Zaria's waist into mine
plus this peppermint tea will keep me together
we glance up at the hallway clock
all at once
under the sound of the one-minute
warning bell slapping us

back into regents reality

we all shake hands
wish each other
good luck

all the luck in the world will not save you

if you don't remember these instructions   listen carefully:
you can only fill in the answer bubbles with a number-two pencil
not a Sharpie   not your favorite gel pen   not a crayon
a well-sharpened number-two pencil filling the circle   completely

you are to put your first & last name on the top
of ALL of your answer sheets   i will not accept them
stapled together & even if i did accept your stapled pages
it's not my problem if your sheets get loose & mixed up

you are not   under any circumstances allowed
to leave once you've begun taking your test
i don't care if your mother calls you saying

there's a fire in your home   i don't care

you can't open your phone pouches anyway
your test will be disqualified
if you leave this room at any time after
i've placed the sheets on your desk

you could have been taking care of whatever it was
you needed to do in the five-minute
grace period at the beginning of class
but unfortunately for you that's over   godspeed

lastly

& this should go without saying   if you can't keep
                your wandering eyes on your own work
                        for the duration of this test
        you can kiss your chance at passing this class

                                    goodbye

we were freshmen when we thought they'd finally say goodbye to standardized tests

it was 2020 & everything changed making it even harder for most kids
// to sit in a classroom safely   let alone fill in bubbles on answer
sheets // trying to reference information that they'd either missed
or our teachers had // no capacity to teach   Iya & Baba called
it   another plague // said something like it had happened before
but not in their lifetime // & not like this   eventually all our
classes went online & people // were protesting the way anything had
ever been done before

September 2020 was going to be the beginning of our first year in
high school & we were hype // about our newfound independence
that allowed us to leave campus for lunch   choose more
classes   take courses we were curious about just for
fun   but just before a virus changed everything // i was
already starting to discover what a scam it all was // wasn't surprised
that they rushed to get us back in overstuffed classrooms so our
parents // could go back to work   because if our parents didn't
work   achieveachieveachieve // how would there be enough
money for America to keep the rich filthy

what would this country be without forty-hour workweeks & how
would they // be able to teach us that we're nothing if we can't
constantly   produce // there's no use // for any of us if we are
not bodies crowding classrooms // endless hands clamoring for our
teachers' approval // endless cubicles fighting over the next promotion
// people dying so we all can afford to live

all the commotion   the internet   exploding // with
information proving that what Iya & Baba call the hamster wheel
// is trash // we thought the paradigm shift   serious talk
about reparations   the idea of deserved rest for our parents &
later   us // would last // but here we are three years later // back
to normal

normally

i would burn through this test as fast as i possibly could just to spite
somebody // just to prove i'm not as stupid as most of these teachers
think i am   normally // i would loudly flip pages laughing at
the tone & demands that i recall words // that ain't never been in
most of our vocabulary   language posturing as the standard //
for intelligence   normally i would turn my shit in early with a
list of suggested // texts that i know Mr. Schlauss would never call
classic   never ask admin for access to // for the sake of our
attention spans   but today is anything but normal // //

a horrible thunderous bubbling in my gut starts growing   the
uncontrollable urge // to let it go right here in my seat bigger than
me   bigger than any test // bigger than any threat // //

calling Mr. Schlauss's bluff

i find a way to stand up quickly

while i fight the urge
to hold both hands
under me in an
X formation scooting
up toward the front

just beyond Mr. Schlauss's
bagged lunch
& ever present
stack of unread books
on educating inner-city youth

he is hunched over
his iPhone his hands move
an endless swiping left motion
barely pretending to work   his desk now just
another sidewalk where he   hunts for sport

my body makes a quick
L shape up my aisle
& across the front of the class
i clasp both hands around
the doorknob before

making a break for it
down the hallway headed
for the first unoccupied
bathroom i can get to
in just enough time

by the time i make it behind the first stall

my boxers are an embarrassing mess
entire surface of my skin covered in sweat
an unfortunate result of artificial sugar & hot water
on an otherwise empty stomach under stress

i am glad i'm alone here with no one around
to hear my insides exit loudly   echoing
across the bathroom walls   it's all over
in less than five minutes

i unlock the stall door looking both ways
to make sure i'm still the only one
who knows what i've done   able to trash
my soiled underwear in peace

looking at the clock up near the ceiling   i tell myself
i can get back like this tragedy   never happened
finish the exam

with time to spare

only Zaria looks up when i return

Schlauss still at his desk
eyes glued to his phone screen
i slide back into my seat
undetected

with his back turned to us

Schlauss writes FIVE MINUTES
in large lettering
across the chalkboard

Zaria & i have got
our feet up on our desks
our answer sheets facedown

five minutes later
when the dismissal bell
sounds we all gather

our things & head
toward the front to lay
our tests on his desk

with my chest puffed out
my chin to the sky i approach
proud of me   for smashing

yet another exam
that means nothing
as my hand extends toward him

Mr. Schlauss reaches down   near his feet
grabs his empty trash can
lifts it toward my face

& waits

thank you, Cerulean, he says

acknowledging my presence
for the first time all morning

i start to ask him what the trash
can is for & he repeats

THANK YOU, CERULEAN
to which a few others freeze

by the door   i keep my mouth
from dropping to the floor

keep myself from reacting
to another one of his stunts

shit he does to those of us
he doesn't like   for fun

we stand there for far too long
facing off wondering who

will give in   to the other
he tries new words

in case i didn't hear the instructions
behind his statement before:

you can put your test
in here

yo what the fuck is your problem?

i finished my test   with time to spare at that
just like everybody else   i don't see you asking
anybody else in here to do that

        —i also didn't see anybody else sneaking
        out of my classroom in the middle of a test

i had to go to the bathroom, i say through clenched teeth
it was an emergency

        —i know you heard me before we began
        so frankly i don't care   you should have gone

        before you walked into my class & then he
        pulls the sheets from between my fingers

        tears all three of them right down
        the center

whatchu afraid of, huh?

you gotta be afraid of me, fam
afraid to find out i aced that joint
even though you ain't teach us shit
all year?

     i hear the room stiffen
     students standing near the door
     turning to stare at me   at us

afraid to find out i ain't as dumb
as you think i am   capable
of getting up out of here

when all you do is sit behind
your desk with headphones
on your ears   pretending to lesson plan

scrolling Tinder   oh yes
we all   know about what's going on
at home   or should i say

what isn't i pause looking
down at his desk toward
the unlocked phone

an extra-young white girl
smiling through the screen   a heart & an X
below her sparkling teeth

whatchu afraid of, Mr. Schlauss
that if you don't make me look
like i'm the one fucking up

admin will eventually find you out?

that's right

how dare you come at me
when you couldn't even
pass the GRE

      i hear Jai gasp at the door
      Zaria tugs my arm   still silent
      yet begging me to back away

from the war
Mr. Schlauss started & that
i've decided to finish

his face flushes in a way
that tells me he wishes
i'd stop while i'm ahead

      Sara, he says trying to interject
—*Cerulean,* i cut
      whatever   *it looks like you've got*

a lot on your mind, he says
& while i'd love to indulge you
i really don't have time to

be talking about my personal life—
failure or fear—with such
an epic waste

of air

Iya once told me when you can't breathe

you should count:
five things you can see
four things you can feel
three things you can hear
two things you can smell
one thing you can taste

right now there are:
five floating phones filming my face
four hands trying to hold me back
three voices telling me Mr. Schlauss ain't worth it
Zaria's perfume & my sweat stacked under my nostrils
my mouth filling

with spit
accumulated & launched
in Mr. Schlauss's direction
before i shake off all the bodies
trying to subdue me
& storm out

Iya's rec center is far out in Canarsie

so it takes me a good minute to walk through the doors
all the way to the back where the swim instructor lockers are

she's been keeping backup bathing suits in hers
to accommodate the randomness of her firstborn

trunks & a sports bra for me to blow off steam
on any given day after enduring every microaggression

too big to let myself store inside me without
somewhere else to put the rage

i drop in somewhere on the deep end

catch my mama's eye briefly
while she's hunched over
the edge on the shallow side
with a group of toddlers
& their parents

she smiles & winks
toward me realizing
i've discovered the new
pair of red trunks she
bought as a surprise

something to find
on a day like this

all the small kids
clad in floaties in
the water under

her measured voice
squirm in excitement
at the chance to race
each other for the last
five minutes of class

they splash   small arms
                    fighting water
on the other side of the pool

while i begin my laps
feeling Iya's gaze on me

breathing long & deep
knowing she won't ask
just yet why i've left
school this early
in the day

everything looks like night in the deep end

even this early in the day

cracking the water's surface
my body sinks
fast toward
the dark

for seconds i let
all this heavy
plunge me
under

feel the water
give in to all my muscle
remembering
Iya say

muscle is more dense
than fat   the more
muscle
you build

the more the world
is gon' test you
try to pile on more

ignore your pain

make you think you'll

never see the lightness
of the sky again
never leave the ground

until both feet finally
reach the tile with nowhere
else to go
but up

a light press against
the pool floor with arms stretched
to my sides   head tilted back

she doesn't say anything about my day or hers

on the train ride home back uptown
only sits next to me massaging her hands
with peppermint oil the way she's always done

ever since i was old enough
to name the things i could smell
she'd use oil to transport us

somewhere else & suddenly
we weren't on some stuffy subway platform
or walking past a piss-ridden alleyway

we were rubbing our hands together
bringing them to our faces & inhaling
deep until the insides of our nostrils burned

Iya let a few droplets fall
into my palms still saying nothing
reveling in the silence

knowing something's wrong
but not pushing
too soon

as soon as i fall backward

into the fluff of my bed
my phone buzzes
against my thigh like clockwork

Zaria

of course it's Zaria
& i wonder if i'm ready
for the earful

of questioning & scolding
about my temper
my inability

to let things go when teachers
try me   hoping
to get a reaction

Zaria

always the coolest
no matter the confrontation
always calm

no matter the heat

it doesn't matter if i answer now or later

i know she's got heat for me   a mouthful
about our pact & how i was supposed to
hold my head
keep myself together   a mountain
of questions that she already
has the answers to but has to ask
because she's disappointed
in me

yo   where'd you go

you missed the rest of the tests
who knows if any of these assholes
is gon' give you another chance

her face fills the screen
waiting for an answer
some type of explanation

that will make it all make sense
but how do you tell your girlfriend
that you skipped the rest

of your classes to go
for a swim on a day
like this

the center   i'm at home now

                    —&?

& nothing   prolly gon'

go to sleep soon   wassup?

wassup was the first thing i said to Zaria

when i met her

my nerves & intimidation
palpable standing in front
of somebody seemingly so
unbothered & beyond
this world

i was putzing around
SoHo with Irv & Jai
looking for jeans
graphic tees & beanies
at some boutique store

we'd never been to

she was restocking
bougie curated clothing racks
then was behind the register
then again standing
at the door

on our way out saying goodbye
Jai pointed out the fact
that she'd been eyeing me
through her red-tinted
sunglasses

always

just an earshot away from us
& our then-clueless
conversation about what might
look good draped across
my broad shoulders

& too-long limbs
her gently making
suggestions at each corner
of the store subtly becoming
a welcome upgrade

you not worried about your grades?

she questions   eyebrows furrowed
full of concern i sometimes grow tired of

i mean   *worried is subjective*
you mean worried   *like scared*

or worried   *like i care about the impact*
of my actions   i ask, trying to emphasize

words Mr. Schlauss thinks
i don't know nothin about

cause, baby, i ain't never scared
i joke trying to jerk a smile out of her

Zaria says nothing   continuing to pace
her magazine-cover-filled room   with Black women's faces

donning avant-garde hairstyles along the walls
peeking from behind her body while she searches

for words that she thinks i'm more
likely to listen to   this is us

both appearing opposite
of our regard for the rules

i   a self-contained, genderfluid nerd
with total irreverence for authority

her   a wild Afrofuturist video vixen

unconvinced of her ability

to let a ball drop

or a thing go

i say lingering a few seconds more
making sure when i hit the end call button
i won't be accused of hanging up on my girlfriend
when all i wanted was a minute to be with my thoughts:

i don't ever want to see that piece of shit
they say is my teacher again
but we are still six months
from graduation &
i've just made it
ten times
harder

to leave

for the rest of the night knowing Jai Irv Zaria Iya Baba will call me
trying to lure me out of bed out of my room downstairs to eat
dinner i won't be able to taste   tired of face-offs with authority
figures who have no place in classrooms let alone school buildings
pretending to teach kids they'd never cough in the direction of
on the street if they weren't getting paid to keep us manageable
docile
obedient
unfree

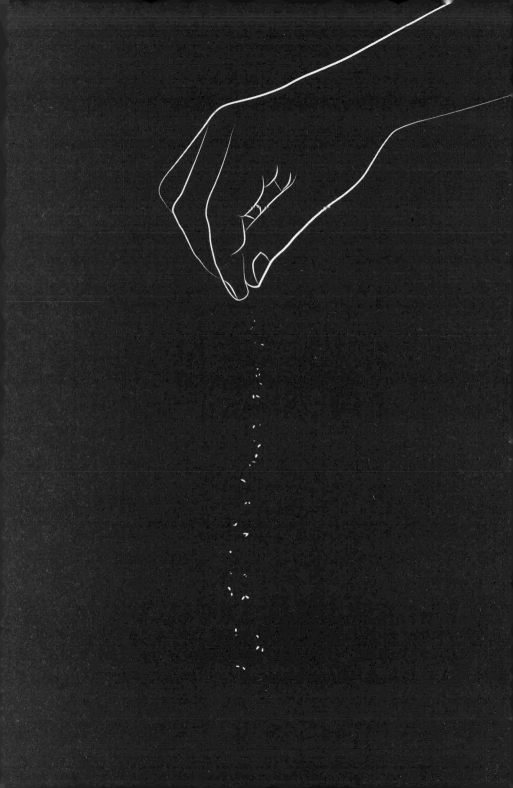

Baba crunches into a slice of toasted challah

drenched in whipped butter & agave jam he made himself
with a pile of opened mail on the opposite end of the kitchen island

he's leaned over it peering into his recipe notebook
studying as if what he's staring at isn't of his own creation

he pushes the extra slice across the countertop without looking up
when i walk into the room   still in my sleep clothes with crust
    in my eyes

even on his off days food is my father's whole life & he is never not
    obsessed
you're going to serve people oatmeal for dinner? i ask stealing

a long look at the list of ingredients & instructions
for tomorrow night's menu at the restaurant he's been at for five years

savory oatmeal, Baby Blue he corrects *it's a whole different experience*
i try to imagine the milky stuff Iya ate for breakfast just a few days ago

on a restaurant table rested on either side of candlelight & i struggle
after they taste this they ain't never gon' want it for breakfast again

spicy andouille, creamy mushroom sauce, & caramelized onion will be
    standard
i still can't picture it but i believe him cause Baba's a culinary genius

i'm sorry, Baba, but that sounds like a big bowl of brown mess i press
reminding him of what he taught both me & Airyn a long time ago:

a dish ain't all the way there if it lacks enough color   you gotta eat
   the rainbow

now how you gon' try to school the teacher? Baba asks with a smirk
sliding the notebook across so i can see the rest of the recipe close up

he plans to top it with sautéed dandelion greens & charred grape
   tomatoes
roasted garlic for garnish

speaking of, he says leaning in to make eye contact
aren't you a little late he glances at his watch

around this time don't kids your age have somewhere to be?

Baba didn't go to college

according to Grandma he almost didn't make it out of high school either
your Daddy was a free bird, didn't like nobody measurin his wings

i've seen the pictures of him at my age when he called himself fly
muscled arms draped over the shoulders of girls happy to be near him

setting up shop at all the block parties where he said he charged
five bucks a plate for food his neighborhood wasn't used to

before that he hustled candy on the subway just like kids still do
selling everything to raise money to buy his own ingredients

culinary school was (is) too expensive for a Bronx boy with folks working
graveyard shifts for pennies but my father was after a slice of the chef life

one way or another i have to show Baba i'm just like him:

a dreamer

unable to accept life the way it is
to take no for an answer at every corner
to settle for this normal trajectory
where we just take the disrespect
dismissal & mistreatment
for being human beings from a place
people weren't used to seeing
success stories that aligned
with their narratives & expectations

one way or another i have to show Baba
why i can't go back to that place where
haphazard teachers can just determine
you fail because you diverge from their rules

he has to understand that i was just being myself
that i was just taking care of myself
that i was just standing up for myself
that i was just speaking up for myself
& that means

i had no other choice
no matter what promise or pact
i made with anyone else
no matter how selfish
it may have seemed

Baba is waiting for me to explain my choice to be home today

already knowing that me being late means i'm not going at all
he leans farther onto the counter in the way he always does
to show us that he's listening to whatever we have to say
the challah toast is in our bellies now & there is nothing
between us but a mostly empty plate of small crumbs
deep breaths
heavy silence

i was thinkin about that story you told me
a couple years ago i start, calculating my words
the one about how you became a chef for real
the hoops you had to jump through & allat
he stares at me wondering where i'm going with this
what it has to do
with right now

his lifted eyebrow tells me to go on
& last night i had a dream about what i want
in the dream i was in an open field surrounded
by all these flowers &, not too far from me,
there were plots of land with fruits & vegetables
a big yellow barn
& a bright green house

built with my own hands

he settles back onto his stool with his elbows on the counter
placing both hands under his chin folded together

Irv & Jai & Zaria were there too
each of them taking care of something different
on the land & i was staring up at the sky
the clouds moving
farther from me

all the surrounding trees grew higher & higher
like they would never stop

it felt important

Baba, i don't think i'll ever be able to get to that place
or even ever feel like that if i go back to that school right now

that school is eating me alive

he sounds so alive when he laughs

first it sounds like a deep rumbling
then a desperate wheeze until it turns
into a full-blown cackle coupled with coughs
in between which he gasps for air
as he leans forward in his chair
with one fist clenched barely covering
his gap-toothed mouth

wow, i see what you just did there
he says, finally catching his breath
your mama know about all of this?
he asks, finally clearing his throat
    not yet, i tell him, trying to read this reaction
    we didn't really talk on the way home

we know about yesterday, he says
the school called when you went upstairs
they won't let you go back right now   *anyway*

Blue, we know what happened

everyone knows what happened

the parents got a phone call from the school
the school told the parents the behavior was

inappropriate   *something that won't be tolerated*   *unacceptable*

the school suggested three weeks of suspension
& closed campus lunches when *the child* returns

these parents asked what will happen to the teacher
for talking to *their child* like that   for treating *their child* like that

for escalating things

the school defended the teacher's responsibility
to hold *the child* accountable to the standards

the school defended the teacher's right
to give consequences where they are due

out of control   *trouble with authority*   *disrespectful*

are the words the school used when describing
the child & why this has happened

Baba tells me all this cause he wants me to know
Baba tells me this cause in this house there are

no secrets & we are on the same side

my tears aren't a secret

as i swing open the fridge door

search for the cartoon of eggs
crack three open into a large
bowl to whisk with
black pepper
pink salt

my tears aren't a secret

as i chop red onion
a clove
of garlic
shred
parmesan cheese

my tears aren't a secret

nor is the fact that i cry
when i'm angry
feeling explosive
toward every adult
who doesn't

understand me
or my friends
or what matters
to us
& our lives

my tears aren't a secret

in front of Baba as i melt
butter in the pan
let it brown a little
pour egg mix above the fire below

sprinkle in the veggies
the cheese
let it bubble
move it
watch it thicken

my tears aren't a secret to myself

but they come back so quick
the omelet i'd flip
with ease
on any other day
turns scramble

my tears aren't a secret

i convince myself
this is what happens
when you're meant
to become
something
else

not going to school doesn't mean there isn't something else

all of us keep hustles
to earn us the means to be

independent

from our parents
from institutions

hustles we've had almost
since freshmen year when we

realized

we needed to get up out of here
or at least do things different

mine is essays   Zaria's is retail
Jai's is paintings   Irv's is candy

all of us: random errands
for local barbershops and salons
& elders too old to brave the stairs at their apartments

my anarchist academic game
is too strong not to capitalize on

no matter how much
Mr. Schlauss has tried to make it seem

like i don't know anything   no one
in the senior class can string a sentence together

better than Cerulean Gene

no one can write these teacher-pleasing papers
with more covert strategy than an enby

smart enough

to attract student clients with funds willing
to pay the price to make sure they

receive a B or higher
every time

the grades vary to dodge teachers
pressed to flag this age-old scheme

so when kids started asking me for help
i began helping a little more than usual

something us queer kids know well:
how to shapeshift into others' voices

here   under the disguise
of reluctant tutor

banished to study hall detention
for kids who couldn't seem

to apply themselves

recipe for writing essays on u.s. history like a kid who applies themself as demonstrated by Mr. Schlauss who was also assigned to teach u.s. history because P.S. 5000 is understaffed

You Will Need:

at least two time stamps that span the past four hundred or so years
a heavy pour of old white men's names who've been made into monuments
a handful of words like   *parliament   president   unprecedented   past*

at least five paragraphs including an introduction proving you read a book you hate
one conclusion to restate the bullet points you found in a chapter of that same book you hate
one thesis statement with a claim that you're not sure about yet but your teacher agrees with

at least three more claims to support your thesis about a system that includes *justice for all & enemies of the state* instead of structures creating enemies
or situations where people just end up having to do what they gotta do

one *therefore* two *moreover*s four *thusly*s at least one *based on my findings*
500–750 words put together to validate & justify the English language
as many nods to the fact that your teacher has done their job

as you can

you can see the drama on Jai's face

from down the hall
where they lean against their locker talking shit after the final bell
with Irv & Zaria whose backs are turned to me
until Jai gasps then screams at the local outlaw
making an appearance inside the school building
even though everybody knows i'm suspended

they ain't really say
i couldn't be here outside
school hours & i
don't plan to be here for more
than five minutes anyway

in about four smooth movements
i slap hands with Irv
scoop Jai off their feet into a hug
push a kiss into Zaria's neck
she winces, her face   stone
at the sight of me
i unzip a girl's backpack   Keisha Caldwell
slip her folder with the essay
she asked me to take care of
back inside it in passing   she grins
a silent *thank-you* & we head out
before i'm noticed
by any teachers
with nothing
but time

Zaria's been giving me the stiff arm

but i reach for her hand anyway
our fingers are usually interlaced
when the group is out gallivanting
through the city looking
for some cool shit to do
unlike most of the kids in our borough
who never go past
the Bronx Bridge never
transfer from the 1 train
to any other line
never known anything beyond
grand concourse shopping
chopped cheese on a roll
sidewalk hookah parties
never go below 138th street
to witness
skin color
style
stance
lifestyle
c   h   a   n   g   e
the more you move deeper
into the rest of the 8.4 million
that pack this city
i reach for Zaria's hand
in the quick busyness of it all
as we move through Harlem
farther down Manhattan

toward Brooklyn
& she
keeps her face
forward
shifts both of her hands
into her lap
hand-holding
is for people
who are together
for people who keep   *promises*   *maybe pacts?*
she says
you only think
about yourself

people always believe you only think about yourself

when you do something they don't like or that they think is chaotic
they think going off in front of "mixed company" or saying no to some
    arbitrary
rules is you just unable to keep control of yourself for the greater good
of the group   say   you are *selfish reckless wild doing too much*
but what they don't understand is if one of us doesn't resist   if
one of us doesn't check folks who think they can talk any kind of
way to us   these people will walk all over us for the rest of our lives
these people   will mess with all of us   out of spite   people
always believe you only think about yourself when you go off script
make a decision that was unplanned   & what they don't understand
is that i was sending a message

for the sake of us all

all of us are strangely quiet

still under the whip of Zaria's irritation
with me & my decision-making
as we exit the train just before reaching
the cusp of Manhattan & Brooklyn Bridge

we always visit Baba on Canal Street
before heading to the open mic in Bed-Stuy
a scene where we're surrounded by
people like us

Baba is already flush with sweat
a faint ring of dampness pooling
around the edge of his chef's hat
as he dishes out instructions to

line cooks sous chefs & the rest
of the dinner service staff at
Country Table Afrique
Baba's dream playground

pride & joy
a place
where he always jokes
he gets money

playing with his food

yo hook us up with something to eat Baba

i say with a hand grazing my belly
standing before him at the restaurant entrance
my friends linger behind me with innocent
looks on their faces the way we always do
when trying to get whatever scraps they might
throw us from last night's service

we've been trying this for years & it rarely
gets us anywhere   Baba always reminding us
this place of business has class & none of y'all
pass for anybody on staff   *i love you but no*
we all groan & take the short lap through
the dining room to the kitchen to the pantry
back to the front as always   sniffing   looking   wishing

though our interest in the space dwindles now
that we know we won't be getting anything for free
still the tingle of minced garlic the burn of onion
steam rising from pots boiling & pans frying above large blue flames
make our mouths water & our eyes widen
at the delicious show of it all *y'all go on now*
Baba says *have fun & make sure you eat*
before you get home he says

tucking a twenty-dollar bill into my hand
to help me take care of myself
he looks across the space full of empty
tables & chairs soon to be buzzing with demands

already tired from a shift that's just
at the beginning   aware
that we'll both get home late
happy but tired

Baba is happiest inside a kitchen

just like i'm happiest
being left alone to create
my own reality with my friends
exploring
imagining a life lived
without the threat of being
seen as worthless
if you don't achieveachieveachieve
on somebody else's terms

Baba is happiest being swarmed
with dinner service orders
voices naming
the choreography of how to survive
a busy kitchen during a rush
screaming:
behind
behind
behind
yes chef
corner
corner
corner

yes chef
behind!

at utica uncut open mic

Irv reads a poem about some intergalactic space world that none of
us really understand // but it sounds good // the way he flips & plays
with words on a level we haven't even seen most rappers achieve
// he weaves in all the vocab he picks up from his favorite books //
things he learned from people he calls his OGs // like Octavia Butler
N. K. Jemisin Kwame Mbalia Marlon James // Black science fiction
writers he reveres even though Irv rather write poems // says he likes
that he don't have to use too many words even though he loves to learn
new ones // springs them on us in the middle of regular conversation
just for fun // always reminding us that i'm not the only one with
brains in the group // that he too can be a mastermind strategist in our
big after-high-school life plans // but before we talk about all that later
// all of us just watch him remembering why we ever became friends //
all of us dreamers refuse to accept this world without changing how it
ends

our night out ends at a specialty samosa spot around the corner

before we hop back on the train for the long commute back to our homes
here we've met most weeks after the open mic for the past six months or so
here the owner is now so used to seeing us that we usually can score an
    extra round

on the house

he always lingers a bit over our spread of notebooks pens maps
    drawings
making inquisitive sounds that we never really lean into
    reminding him   this plan
is top secret meaning only for us

over three kinds of samosa: beef curry   chicken tikka   & veggie
all of us spend the first part of our time daydreaming aloud
    what we look forward to
most & how each of our hustles is going before we get into

the hard stuff

recipe for living off the grid as told by Google
serves 4

You will need (to find):

your own food
your own shelter
your own water source
your own source of power

to practice no longer letting our phones control us

we'd all put ours in Jai's bag just before we walked in to focus on our plans
every week on this day the rule is the same: no phones until we're home
all of us take it seriously since it wasn't some teacher's stupid idea

this way of doing things belonged to us
we began to own the life we said we wanted
& it became our small source of power

everybody gon' miss us y'all, watch Jai informs the table
they then go on to remind us that they won't be missing *everybody*
that Jai's big sister never really understood Jai anyway

that, though things were okay at their house, it's still good riddance
to having to explain themself or endure endless looks of confusion
about what they were wearing listening to reading making

on their sewing machine in the middle of the night   the only time
they were free of what they called Heteronormative Interruptions™
i'm ready to be all the things everywhere baby, they say

motioning their arms like they're creating a rainbow out of thin air
high-fiving Zaria &, with the other hand, scrunching their hair
Sis really gon' miss all this color up in that dry-ass house

they say   & we all nod   in agreement

156

for me, it's all about the aesthetic

palm trees
mountains
open grass
short walks
to the beach
crystal shops
top-tier weed

Zaria's mother
is a hippie, like
a real one, like
seventies real, except
fifty years behind
in her own world
on her own time

free love
psychedelics
wild hair
flowers plants
everywhere
& allows Zaria
to do anything

but for her
that meant
missing almost
everything

Zaria wanted
her to see
she prolly
won't even
notice
i'm gone

Zaria says slipping out
of the impersonation
she prolly been
counting down
the days
to being
childless again
all along

or maybe
she'd be
sort of proud
her baby
finally fully
followed
in her selfish footsteps

nodding to what everybody in the group says
they're excited about finding Out West
there's not much moving but his chest & head
his mouth strangely staying closed
when normally he'd be the one with the most
to say about the best ways to plot our escape
from the everyday societal grind

i stare into the side of his face
same way i always do
when he zones out the way
he does every once in a while
where none of us could say where
he goes in his head taking his time
to come back

he scribbles something down
on a napkin then folds it over & over
leaning forward to stuff it into his
back pocket without sharing
he eventually turns to look back at me
a bashful smile spreading across
his face as always

you got a staring problem?
he asks, poking at me

nah, you got a secret?

it's no secret that Irv grew up a lot different than me

than all of us

still it's a little bit
of a mystery
what happens
when he goes home
day to day
we've just always
hung out at my place
sometimes at Zaria's
her mother
dubbing herself
a cool mom
who always says
she'd rather us
do whatever
under her roof

truth is we still
don't know
what it's like
at Irv's
never really
needed to know either
cause Irv loves
his space

& won't

none of us
disrespect that
don't none of us
ever cross
each other's
lines

whatchu excited about?
i ask him

he tells me: *having a dream*
that's mine

BE MINE . . . OR ELSE

FOR A GOOD TIME
CALL . . . YOUR MOM
POOP EVERY POOP
LIKE IT'S THE END
OF THE WORLD
POOP
LIKE YOU HAVEN'T
SEEN A TOILET
IN WEEKS
GO HOME DAD
YOU'RE DRUNK
YOUR DAD IS A NICE DUDE
YOUR DAD IS A DILF
NOBODY SAYS DILF YOU
REVERSE MISOGYNIST
YES WE DO YOU
REAL MISOGYNIST
THE WORLD NEEDS
YOUR POOP
DREAM BIG

THE WORLD
IS YOUR BUTTHOLE

all of us already know
even though the samosa spot
got some of the best food

162

using any of their bathroom stalls
puts you at risk
of secondhand funk
random unidentified smears
along the walls
witnessing Sharpie arguments
between New York City strangers
Zaria grabbed my hand
to stop me
but i still went in there thinking
this time i was too full of mango lassi
to care
i draw a heart
around the part that says
YOUR DAD IS A NICE DUDE
with my own Sharpie
before deciding to hold my pee
til i get home

like i should have done in the first place

back home on the toilet i power my phone back on

then wait for it to light up like a fiend // immediately // it begins
buzzing nonstop // which isn't that weird for a phone that's been
turned off for almost four hours // & so // i wait for the chaos in my
hand to eventually stop // the screen // fills with notifications from
Airyn then Iya // thirty-two texts // fifteen calls // three voicemails
being the worst of it // the actual cause for alarm // my hand moves up
my chest reaching for something to hold on to // because don't nobody
leave voicemails no more // you don't leave voicemails unless //
something's wrong // an emergency // maybe somebody died   an
explosion   maybe finally // America is finally receiving its karma
& we have to flee // whatever it is // something has happened // i'd left
the bathroom door wide open // expecting everybody in the house //
to be asleep // & suddenly i wonder if really // no one is here // i flush
the toilet & wash my hands // go running down the hall to Airyn's
room // fling the door open

empty

run across to Iya & Baba's room   hear a voice blaring
from the living-room tv
behind me now far off   something i didn't notice until closer
to my parents' door

who has what it takes . . . to survive on their own? who will conquer the
dangers of this wild land?

empty

i get up the courage to pull up the very last voicemail from Airyn //

press play wincing at the tremble in his voice // him attempting to

sound mature // to give me the facts

all i can hear is:

Blue, it's Bubby, hurry
pick up your phone
i don't know what is happening
but it's bad

my stomach   empties

& i'm
scared

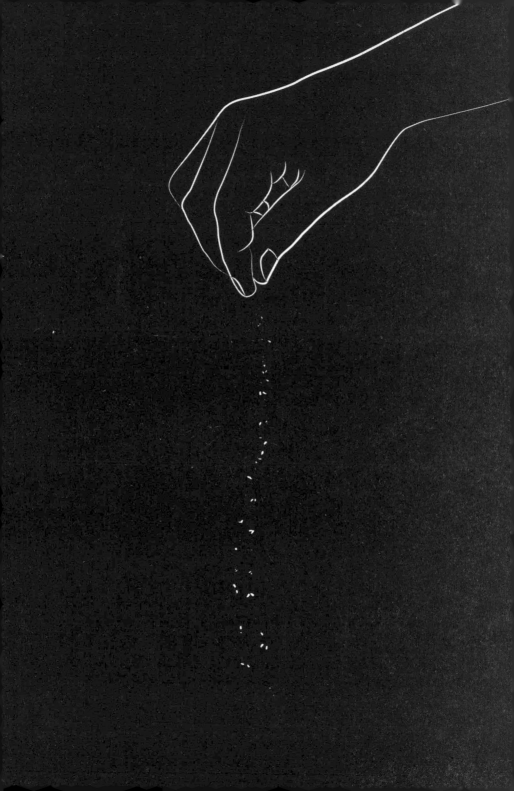

hospitals I.

are all
blinding light
beeping machines
wheelchairs
faces so long
they touch
the ground

are all
family must
wait here
the doctor
would like
to speak
with you
now

are all
antiseptic wipes
the smell of bleach
saline bags
morphine
& other
drugs
to numb
unthinkable
pain

are all
cannot
look
cannot
deal
cannot
believe
it's my
father
outstretched
eyes closed
not moving   in that bed

hospitals II.

are all
can you push
one more time
for me

are all
you're almost
there   soon   we will see
the head

were all
she's lost a lot of
blood   she's tired
but we're so close

were all
move   out the way
fetal heart rate
dropped

were all
baby must
come out
right now

were all
beeping machines
Iya's body doing the most
to stay alive

for a world   and a baby
who can't
guarantee they'll
return the favor

hospitals
are where you come
unsure of who will die
& what will be born

Baba & Iya say Airyn was determined to enter the world too soon

say he couldn't wait to climb out of our mama
so he could get to work on the next world

say Iya couldn't tolerate much of what
used to be her favorite things to eat

say the smells began to send her body into sickness
make her lightheaded & nauseous

say the doctor had to keep watch on her
bursting body far before Airyn was due &

say she banned Baba from cooking with garlic
say the scent she once loved turned stench in her nostrils

say the magic that we were so used to filling
our house with warmth soon became what she complained of most

from bed rest to my brother's birth

Baba's bed is pushed all the way to the back

of a large beige room behind an equally large blue curtain next
to a wall-to-wall window where he almost looks like he's not
breathingbreathingbreathing & almost like he really wouldn't if there
weren't all those wireswireswires connected to a beige computer
screen with all these digitsdigitsdigits connected to his chest & then
to the inside of his elbow & then his wrist & then a longlonglong
tube that goes from a large box pushing airairair to his nostrils
helping him hold on & the doctors come in & out checking his
pulsepulsepulse making sure that
he's
       still
            alive
my brain tells me the man in the bed is nothing but a mummy
& absolutely not my baba cause the man in the bed looks
nothingnothingnothing like him he is just way too wrapped in
loose gauze needing too much helphelphelp with his arms being
heldheldheld midair by slings taped to his hands so as not to pressure
his blistering arms while keeping them from touching anything
around him to keep them from hurting more than they already do
maybe to keep him from
falling
      all the way
           apart
no one is talking to me really & Iya is just pacing the room & Airyn
is in the corner with his knees to his chestchestchest his face so wet
& frozen staring at Baba wishing he would just wakewakewake up
already say something do something open his eyes & tell us all of this

is just some type of Halloween costume some extra-early April Fool's
joke move something to make us believe that
the worst

     isn't

          true

the truth is it could have been a lot worse

Dr. Pierce says to all of us standing around the edges
of Baba's bed as he continues to rest unmoving under our breath
the beeping of all the machines pulling me in & out of
words she uses like

kitchen fire   *2nd degree burns*   *both arms*   *coma*

we could have lost him she says while i'm still not convinced
we haven't   he hasn't moved since i got here & through
my tears he looks like nothing more than a mirage masquerading
as my favorite person in the world

we could have lost him but he made it out just in time for it
not to affect the nerve endings more deeply in his arms or his
chest she says as if she's talking about someone she actually knows
says "we" as if losing this person would change *her* whole world

she says *right now he just needs to rest & let the meds take effect*
she says *he's got a long road to recovery, but recovery isn't impossible*
she says *he will need a lot of support, but he will pull through*

in no time

for what feels like the one millionth time Iya bursts into tears

while covering her face with both hands in the arms of Uncle Charlie
                              Baba's best sous chef
he tries to comfort her, tell her everything will for sure be all right & he
                              was right there
tells us things moved so fast, the way everything lit up
                              seeing it all happen
was terrifying but not too unfamiliar even though this was a first
                              in their kitchen
he tells us he dodged the pan of hot oil but not the open flame
                              after the collision
a line cook was wearing earbuds & didn't hear Baba say *BEHIND*
                              trying to get past
all the fast-moving preparations for a busy night, he tells us that
                              everyone cooking
froze as they were trained to do when something dangerous happens
                              in attempts to reduce
the possibility of anyone getting injured even though it was too late
                              the size of the flames
already towered over Baba & instinctively, his outstretched arms
                              & exposed skin
reached into the growing fire that quickly ran up him in seconds
                              needing to be put out
                              by several cooks
                              removing their jackets
                              covering him to calm
                              the blaze
                              the beast

Baba had long ago described the nature of the culinary beast

had told us more stories about dicing pounds of veggies to make
gallons of stock than Airyn & i knew what to do with // had taught
us the proper ways to hold knives having known firsthand how
easily one could slice a finger // land // on a toe // had reminisced in
our living room with Uncle Charlie about the first time they'd ever
roamed around a stainless steel counter finding their places back in the
assembly lines // been yelled at // embarrassed in front of the entire
staff by the executive chef at the smallest mistake // slightest second of
daydreaming // even too much unfocused talking during a dinner rush
// Baba had told us so many times of the dangers he'd faced as a wide-
eyed newbie to this culinary land // how it'd tried him over & over
again // made him want to quit & still return the next day // given he'd
invested everything into his plan // had only ever been out // for a day
here // & a day there // for minor injuries // swollen feet from hours &
hours of standing back to back

but nothing
had ever been as bad

                        as this

just hours ago Baba donned his white coat pressed smooth as ever

where we stood checking in with each other at the doors of Country
    Table Afrique
he looked the way he always does in his uniform, comfortable content

            happy

this was his dream: to be head chef for a restaurant that he believed in
a place he felt proud of presenting the food to people he'd never met
    before

                everything

was an experience that was bigger than most people where we're from
    could ever
imagine or expect from the likes of Us, which was Baba's true specialty:
    proving   everyone

                wrong

nothing seemed like it could go wrong   nothing

                felt
out

of

                    place

```
          nothing        felt
          outofplace              nothing
                                  felt
                                  out
                                  of
                                  place
```

just hours ago
seeing Baba in his
chef's coat
freshly shaven
his skin gleaming
so smooth
with the shiniest
smile above
the smallest
goatee beaming about
barbecued baked bean stew
mini okra gumbo potpies
sweet potato salad
peach cobbler coulis
Uncle Charlie & all
his line cooks already
slicing boiling stewing
baking frying blending
him beaming about
how everything
is working
in perfect
order

recipe for the beginning of things falling apart

you will need:

one empty house with every light left on & things running
two siblings left to care for themselves for the night
several questions about what happens next after
one parent has gotten hurt &
another parent starts hurting
trying to hold things together

you will need:

to find ways not to panic in front of your little brother
to find ways to panic in the dark behind your bedroom door
to find ways to not worry about how bad it might get
to find ways to think ahead if things get as bad as they can
to find ways to be a person again when you start to go numb
to find ways to stop being a person & let the feelings breathe

you will need:

two feet to pace the house
a couch to collapse in
a phone dying dead left where you sat it down
a world that doesn't stop because something bad has happened to us
lots & lots of quiet quiet silence silence silence being so still
the space to not leave your house   to not speak to anyone

for days

what is it with everyone & the need to always have access to me

my thoughts
my body
my things

something must be wrong with you
if you don't want to answer
the phone

something must be wrong with you
if you ignore
notifications

want   to be   alone

you must be
helping hands
mastermind

or slave

to constant buzzing
ringing
clocks
screens
likes
comments
shares

to the world   those

are not the problem
are not the real issue:
the weirdo is you

because there isn't
enough space
in your head
your heart
your limbs

to give a fuck about anything
but what's going to happen
to your family
now

you got 132 texts on your phone right now, Blue?

Bubby, i—

—that's way too much
your friends are gonna
ghost you
like you doin
to them, watch
Airyn warns me
from the edge
of my bed
while my face
stays
pressed
into the
dented belly
of my pillow
wondering who
taught my brother
the word *ghost*

i don't have to sit up to see how scrunched his face is when he says this
the way his small fingers scroll my phone screen finally turned back on
after
i don't know how   l   o   n   g

i don't have to talk about it with him to understand the meaning
behind his words:
you're being weird & you need to talk & tell them what is going on
with Baba   with Us
even if you don't really have the words yet

Blue, it's really bad
Zaria Jai Irv
are all starting to
type in all caps
& that couldn't
be good
don't worry
i won't open
none of them

even though
you look kinda dead
you'd prolly
still pop me

but on some real stuff:
you probably should at least
get up & wash   your butt

**shower steam overtakes the bathroom while i hover above my
phone screen**

YO . . . WHERE YOU BEEN AT FAM?

BABE . . . WE NEED TO TALK

OH SO YOU NOT TALKING TO *ME* NOW
ALRIGHT, BET

CERULEAN THIS IS GETTING CHILDISH.

ARE WE GON' TALK OR NOT
WHAT'S UP WITH YOU SIB
YOU WASN'T AT OUR SPOT
YESTERDAY & YOU STILL
NOT ANSWERIN THE PHONE

FAM, ARE YOU GOOD?!

HEARD ABOUT YOUR POP, SIB
CAME BY YESTERDAY &
YOUR MOMS SAID YOU WAS
ASLEEP

TEXT ME WHEN YOU GET THIS

AYE FAM   WE WORRIED
ANYTHING WE CAN DO
TO HELP

SO YOU JUST GONNA
KEEP LOCKING ME OUT

I THOUGHT WE TALKED
ABOUT EVERYTHING

SAY SOMETHING
PLEASE

I'M NOT MAD AT YOU
NO MORE

        WE JUST WANT EVERYTHING TO BE OK

to the group:

my bad y'all
got a lot of shit
goin on

Baba had
an accident
he gon' be all right tho

hope y'all
good
is all i have to say

when i finally get out the shower it's night

my skin looks like i've been underwater all day
pruned & sucked dry of so much color
the house is still & i shiver walking down
the hallway in my towel   droplets falling
from my locs down my back & legs

i can hear Iya's quivering voice in the kitchen
her words muffled most likely by a hand loosely
held over her mouth as she speaks to Baba on the phone
we can always tell when she is speaking to Baba
unable to fully make out what she's saying

i overhear the strange tone Iya speaks with
a few words at a time coming through like:
we'll figure it out, baby   *we always do*
don't worry about that right now   *you'll be back*
in no time   *it hasn't even*   *been that long*

after all these years   *this ain't gonna be*
what stops you

Iya's back straightens at the sight of me stepping into the dining room

where she looks small & ethereal under the dim light cast over her
head & shoulders like a halo // she is now an angel responsible
for turning all the papers that cover the table into a simple math
equation // responsible for making sure things keep moving along
as they should // she quickly wipes the wet from her face & smiles at
my emergence somewhat resembling the Cerulean she knows // *my
baby* she says // *you smell like lavender & vanilla* // *i couldn't think of
a better time than this for you to be stealing the last of my shower gel*
// she caught me but she isn't mad // by the softness in her face i can
tell she is all relief & no objection to me // taking what i need // *Airyn
basically told me i stink* // *so i had to do what i had to do* // i joke // say
// *i figured he might be right this time* // still trying to appear as fine as
possible // Iya shuffles all the documents spread across the table // into
two neat piles // sticking Post-its in between sections // says // *Baba's
coming home very soon*

twenty days for twenty percent of his body

according to doctors
when a body is burned
bad as Baba's was
you can expect to stay
one day for every percent
of skin the fire stole
there will be regular
antibiotic applications
around the clock
creams prescribed
so the body doesn't
get even sicker with
open flesh exposed
to the air's elements

in between

doctors will come
to clean the wounded
surface of the body
replace soiled bandages
with new ones needing
change again
just hours later
provide the body
with electrolytes
pain medications
monitoring for infection

after twenty days

Baba comes home
with strict instructions
to keep wounds clean
then keep them
moisturized
once they close
to avoid scars
to rest
to rest
to rest

i guess the rest is all i can think about:

how Baba has always been everything // how Baba has always been
the light at the end of the tunnel // & every comparable cliché there
is to say // my father is always the one we run to when something
goes wrong // to tell us that everything will be okay // to remind me
who i am // to show me what it looks like to be what everyone calls
impossible // imperfect // immovable // when the world says i can't i
shouldn't i won't i better not // i guess the rest is all i can think about //
how Baba always knows what Iya needs & never waits for her to have
to ask // how Baba lets all of us take the lead but never made us feel
like we had to // how he was the first to teach me how to say *Fuck You*
to the patriarchy // even though he still has his own unlearning to do
// how Baba always sat alongside Iya when i'd come home from school
with scrapes cuts bruises from being myself on the playground //
together they'd clean it cover it kiss it // tell me time & care heals all //
& now // i will have to return every favor // now // it is me //
who Baba needs to break //
the fall

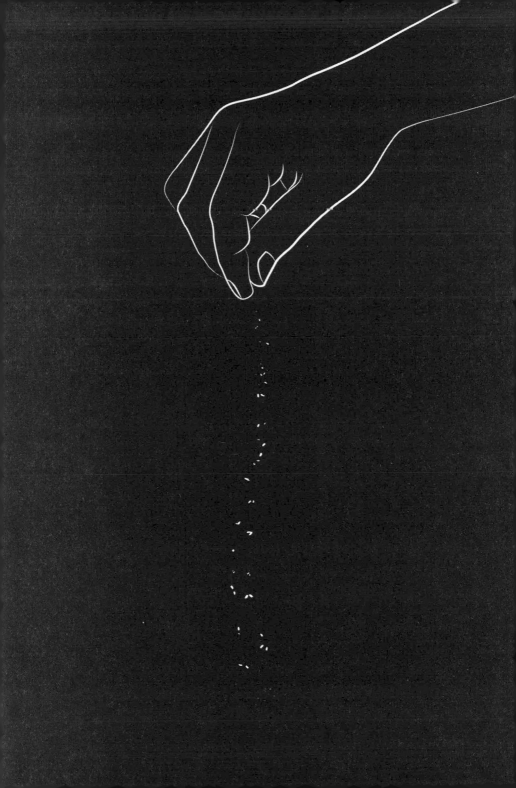

OFFICE OF THE PRINCIPAL

P.S. 5000 BRONX FUTURES INSTITUTE
BRONX, NY
10466

RE: SCHOOL ABSENCES (NOTICE #3)

Dear_____ Mr. & Mrs. Gene _____,

The New York City Department of Education (DOE) mandates a maximum of ten (10) excused absences, per student, per school year. This also includes tardiness in excess. All children are marked tardy, whether he/she is late to school, or leaving early.

Your child, _____ Cerulean Gene _____, has now been absent from school for _____ 26 _____ days. This is our _____ 3rd _____ formal attempt at reaching you. You must call the school immediately to schedule a meeting with Principal Krumer to explain these absences at this time. Medical absences do not count against the ten days allowed in the year. But if your child is ill for more than five (5) consecutive days, verification from a doctor is required for reentry.

Children learn best when they are in school consistently. However, if circumstances at home prevent him/her from attending school as mandated, counseling services will be recommended for you.

We hope to hear from you soon.

Bronx Futures Staff

i fold the letter two times

placing it back into the envelope it came in
toss it into the small tray of everythings
Iya & Baba keep on the kitchen counter

for whenever they feel like allowing
the noise of outside in to affect what's
going on here with all of us

notice it growing fuller taller wider every day
that i am home with Baba blowing off the world
like nothing else matters because it doesn't

i chuck my jacket onto the couch & place
a bag of groceries onto the counter
walk into the dark crevice that is my parents' bedroom

now that it's been rearranged for Baba's comfort:

a mound
of soft pillows
a side table
of ointments
ice packs
medicines
remote controls
snacks
a dresser
shifted closer

to the bed
for easy
access
to loose
clothes

Baba begins
talking to me
the minute
he hears me
enter even
though he doesn't
look

look, ain't nobody gone have me on no island in 2024

it's already crazy as hell out there
& people signing up
to be dropped off in the middle
of nowhere for some contest
to prove they deserve money
that they probably
not gon' win

i feel like that's already life
every time i step
out the door   some contest
with cameras somewhere
with people watching
wondering if i'm gon'
survive

Baba says this while his eyes
float gently toward
his bedside window
his voice trailing off
looking like a sad puppy dog
who's no longer allowed
to go outside & play

i almost feel sorry for him
but it's hard to feel sorry
for somebody who still
talks shit from his bed

& who scooped me up
immediately every time
i fell as a child before

i got a chance to cry

the camera zooms in on a girl with box braids crying

having to endure eating some shit she found in the forest for the one
millionth time on the show // the edited episodes always highlighting
how she's the least cut out for the conditions created // to make them
fail the mission // even though they framed her to be // the one who
needs the reward most // i notice mascara running from her tired eyes
// wonder what she needs that for when she's supposedly out there in
the woods alone // trying to make it back to "civilization" in one piece
// they probably told all the contestants to look their best // remember
// there are billions of people out there // watching // holding their
breaths // probably told them to recall all their deepest traumas fears
insecurities // speak them out loud during tree trunk confessionals //
play up every hard thing so coming back to life as we know it sounds
like the softest place to land // make it seem like ever choosing to leave
the safety & security of our evolved world again would be

irresponsible
impossible
stupid

a lost cause
definitely
too ambitious

for a bunch of teenagers
with nothing
to show for themselves

but some high school diplomas

my stomach drops at the thought of a diploma

as Baba attempts to reach for his own water from the nightstand

i'm grateful for the distraction of being needed by my father
now realizing that the world probably sees dropouts like me
as useless to society with too many weird ideas & an anti attitude
toward everything

at least here right now

i know a person i love needs me if only to keep his throat
from turning to sandpaper or keep his wounds
from turning into mounds of hard clay after a mudslide
of terror

a look of terror flashes across Baba's face

as i sit on his bed blocking the latest episode of *Dystopia Tank Race* to
    lift the straw to his mouth he looks like a helpless baby waiting on
    his parent to quench his helpless thirst

do you need something for the pain i ask him & he tells me *no*
    as he does every time
i cringe watching him try to be strong when he can do
    nothing for himself

it breaks me wishing nothing could ever happen to anybody i love
especially not someone whose whole life has been about protecting me

& his dreams   both of which he can't even lift his arms
to block the world from messing with now

i lift a dry washcloth to Baba's mouth & he knows the bandage change drill:

open wide
bite down
be still
when it hurts
scream
bite harder
when it hurts
focus
on the wall
behind me
when it hurts
trust that
you're held
that this
pain will pass
that you
won't be
stuck
in hell
forever

in thirty minutes Baba's wounds are cleaned & redressed

i wipe the sides of his face where tears
trailed down into his pillow while i moved
as quickly as possible using warm water
to dislodge gauze that refused to part
from his skin without extra effort

i prop a fresh pillow under his neck
watch him drift off into another nap
turning off the TV, i make sure the remote
is within reach for when he
wakes again looking for an escape

i'm not supposed to know it yet but getting hurt is expensive

in a pile next to the regular everyday mail
there's another stack of envelopes all addressed
to Andre Gene from BX Community Hospital Billing Department
i look over my shoulders to remind myself
that Airyn is at school & Iya is all the way in Brooklyn
teaching kids who wouldn't even think about dropping out yet
how to tread deep waters & not drown

Iya has opened every last one of them
placed the bills back in their envelopes almost
as if she's hoping they'll all take care of themselves
i look over my shoulders again & scoop the stack
into my hands, walking the pile over
to the dining table to sit in the exact chair i've seen her in
pretty much every night since Baba's accident

thousands of dollars for anesthesia during treatment
thousands of dollars for sleeping in a hospital bed overnight
hundreds of dollars for painkillers you could buy in a bodega
hundreds more for painkillers you couldn't
every small thing on a long list done to make Baba comfortable
becoming a big thing that feels like it's changed the little comfort

he once brought to all our once-simpler lives

adult lives seem like they're all about work

once it's not

the world
sees you
as useless
pitiful
someone who
should be
ashamed
for not being
able to
provide
able to
prove
your worth

the earth
though soft
& thick
with soil
a harsh place
to live when you
have kids
& other
never-ending
responsibilities
that make

adults slaves
to money

to whatever
will pay

the bills

my belly screams at me

trying to understand these digits & dollar signs while i still haven't eaten // it's easy to forget about food when life is suddenly this bland // every day // Baba & i have our routines where i am just at his service // it is now my job // to make sure he eats drinks is clean after he uses the bathroom // since he can't do anything with his own hands // it's easy to be off food when your stomach is just a bunch of // tangled-up noodles unchewed // until they are gummed together at the center of your chest // the tangling growing so full & uncomfortable that it feels like nothing else can fit anywhere in your body // or your life ever again

what you doing with these, baby

these don't look like anything
that concerns you

home early   Iya's voice almost
launches me completely out of my skin

in seconds she's at the dining table
scooping the pile from in front of me

walking to some drawer in the kitchen
stuffing them deep inside

      i was just curious & wanted to see
      what was going on & wanted to see

      how i could help
Iya laughs out loud at me

help what
help how

your job was to stay in school
this here is grown folks' business

this
is for your father & i to worry about

worry about yourself &
what you gon'—

Iya's voice catches in her throat

all of her looking / too tired to finish her sentence / to believe her
sentence / to believe the idea that i keep holding on to: what i will do
next / all my plans feeling so distant from reach now / as if i can think
about that without thinking about Baba being stuck in bed & the world
going on like nothing's happened / like there isn't a wall behind every
wall we knock down / like everything isn't spinning out of control /
rocking us all over the place / while keeping us glued

to the ground

Iya went to college like everybody else in her family

Iya went to college like everybody else in her

Iya went to college like everybody else

Iya went to college like everybody

Iya went to college

Iya went

recipe for finding work in New York City when you're seventeen with no diploma or GED

you will need:

to accept the possibility that you might not be good to anyone
to accept the possibility that you might have to do anything
to accept the possibility that you'll be riding your bike

around the city for hours
& not find anything
realize
you haven't been
anywhere enough
to know the first thing

about what it takes
to get somewhere
new

. . . Ms. Rose says our next assignment is to cook a meal for our
families

that's so stupid

Airyn interrupts my spiral to announce all this
before downing large gulps of chocolate
oat milk out the fridge from the carton

between winded gasps

he's crashed into the kitchen
like some kind of storm
unaware of the heavy quiet before it came

his heart & breath racing
with the excitement of a kid
home from a half day

please don't talk to me
about touching any kind
of food while you still

smell like outside, i say
pinching my nose & fanning
the air in his direction

Airyn's problem
is that he's a gross aloof little kid
who doesn't know what he has

he sees all his school projects
as something all of us got to do
as kids when the truth is

things would be different
if school for me had been anything like his:
beyond passing arbitrary tests

anything beyond worrying
if i have what it takes to survive
what happens **NEXT**

P.S. 5000 BRONX FUTURES INSTITUTE
BRONX, NY
10466

RE: SCHOOL ABSENCES (NOTICE #5)

Dear _____ Mr. & Mrs. Gene _____,

The New York City Department of Education (DOE) mandates a
maximum of ten (10) excused absences, per student, per school year. This
also includes tardiness in excess. All children are marked tardy, whether
he/she is late to school, or leaving early.

Your child, _____ Cerulean Gene _____, has now been absent from school
for _____ 37 _____ days. This is our _____ 5th _____ formal attempt at
reaching you. You must call the school immediately to schedule a meeting
with Principal Krumer to explain these absences at this time. Medical
absences do not count against the ten days allowed in the year. But if
your child is ill for more than five (5) consecutive days, verification from
a doctor is required for reentry.

Children learn best when they are in school consistently. However,
if circumstances at home prevent him/her from attending school as
mandated, counseling services will be recommended for you.

We hope to hear from you soon.

Bronx Futures Staff

II.

ZARIA

when Cerulean Gene first asked me what my name is, they waited
for an answer as if they already knew it. as if they'd seen me before &
were just making sure. they looked at me like it was some sort of test
to see if i would lie to them like the rest of the world had done. & i
wanted to pass the test so bad. i already wanted to be on their good
side. in the few seconds i lingered under the gaze of their furrowed
brows & soft eyes, i hoped i could remember what it said on my birth
certificate. i hoped i'd eventually get to see them without a KN95 mask.
i'd tried to be subtle about following them all around the store & now
was my chance to make sense of it.

to be honest, i didn't really know what it was right away. they just
seemed like they were on their way to somewhere else. the same
way my mama said i do. like there was a haze over their eyes that
told everybody around them they were desperate to get up out of
here. they were ready to go. i was attracted to what it might be like to
imagine another place. another way of being. a whole different life that
suddenly seemed possible just looking at them exist in a small, run-
down fashion boutique here in SoHo. but i couldn't tell them that.

i just told them my name is Zaria & that i liked their T-shirt & invited
them to go spark up in the woods.

a lot of people don't know Pelham Bay Park exists besides it being a train stop

they don't know that if you go across the street
on the other side of the block beyond the tracks, first
sidewalk & patch of grass there's another part
of New York City that's much quieter & less paved

i took Cerulean there on our first date
my backpack stuffed with things that prolly
wouldn't make sense to the average person
but i knew Cerulean wasn't average

watching them from the corner of my eye
as we dodged low branches & extra-wide trees
it felt easy to walk next to somebody
who ain't see none of this nature shit as weird

it was almost like they'd been here before
on their own perched somewhere above it all
watching over a space they knew was special
a space that deserved respect & protecting

when we finally reached a clearing
where we could see both a pathway
to the water beyond a long open fence
& an open area of low grass & tall trees

i asked if we could sit

i could feel Cerulean's eyes searching my skin

while i unloaded the bag:
peanut butter
a large wooden spoon
binoculars
rolling papers
a nug

i could feel Cerulean's fingers
searching my hand
as i guided them
toward a tree
with the spoon
held in the other

i could feel Cerulean's breath
shifting out of curiosity
& awe as they watched me
smooth the peanut butter
in a small opening
in the bark

i could feel Cerulean's heart
quickening
racing
pounding
when we got back
to the log
to sit closer

than we had when we first got there

while i talked about woodpeckers with the binoculars

pressed against my face
Cerulean said they were glad
there wasn't nothin
they were allergic to

nothin that would stop them
from getting whatever
it is they needed
from the earth

that no matter where
they went
they knew
they could survive

now you sound like my mama

y'all know each other? i ask, half serious

sound like her how? they ask me, all serious

*i don't know . . . eating from the earth
& shit like that,* i say, half stealing a glance at them
half waiting to see some movement in the tree

your mama plotting to live off the grid too?

live off the grid? whatchu mean? my body stiffening
for the answer, half of me curious   half of me afraid of what they might
have in common with my mother

*i mean, i don't know that much yet to be honest
i just know i'm not tryna be stuck in a cycle
of following the same rules & paths*

*even though it don't seem like any of it
ever works*

i exhaled hearing something familiar
in their voice that mirrored
something i've always heard in mine

i mean, what you think? Cerulean asked
interrupting a daydream i didn't know
i was having

what do i think about what? & i feel rude

knowing i'd possibly been drifting off

into my own world not listening

to one of the most beautiful people i'd ever seen for a bird

or worse   thoughts about my mama

nah, you missed it, boo   but that's okay

they smirk cutely *&* slip their hands under both of mine

taking control of the binoculars   *i don't blame you*

for not wanting to miss the moment

the woodpecker's artwork feels like the most amazing thing i've ever
seen standing next to Cerulean stoned & eating leftover peanut butter
out the jar // staring into something that didn't exist an hour ago //
we'd scared the bird off with our laughter just minutes after Cerulean
got a chance to see & just before they snuck in a kiss // *i love doing this
with you* they tell me // *what, eating peanut butter in the woods?* i ask //

> *just being away*
> *from everything*
> they said

JAI

usually i don't like nobody staring at me the way Cerulean did when Ms. Rasheed told them to sit next to me in eighth grade. they'd just transferred into my art class & when i finally looked up from my sketchpad, i realized they wasn't doing nothing that everybody else don't do. but when i looked back i saw what they was really staring at was my sketch of Tyler, the Creator on a horse all majestic-like surrounded by flowers just like he would be if he was in a Kehinde Wiley painting. everybody in the class was learning about his portrait style thanks to Deja Collins complaining that all the artists we were learning about were old & white. anyway—i was the only one in the class who could make my shit actually look like his. only one who could match his style of making Black people look natural & regal. only one who could get the colors to shine off the page like he does.

Cerulean asked if i was going to art school like all the other art kids in New York with a look on their face too weird not to answer. so i did. i wanted to know what would come next. now that i know who Cerulean is four years later, the question wasn't weird at all. they was tryna see if i was like them or everybody else. sort of like a friend audition to see if i was as far gone as they were. & by "gone" i mean secretly plotting to somehow escape this sinking ship our parents are leaving us. without looking up from my sketch i asked them why i need to go to college when i've got YouTube & Tyler, the Creator's number in my phone.

we both bust out laughing at the idea of becoming internet famous. i confessed that i really did have a crush on everyone in Odd Future & that i wished i lived in California. that i had dreams of getting to see sunshine every day & paint murals surrounded by palm trees. that money & breaking my sister's heart were the only things stopping me from trying to run away.

you know who that look like?

at first
i planned
to ignore
a question
that sounded
like a setup
for another
one of somebody's
stupid jokes about
which weirdo
i reminded them of

i don't look
like nobody
you ever seen, fam
so don't even
try it
it's only
one of me
i say back
without
looking up

i said
"you know
who THAT
look like?"
not "YOU," they said.

i was talking
about your picture, chill
anyway, that person
look just
like Tyler, the Creator

Cerulean didn't stop there

they asked permission to flip through the rest of my sketchbook's pages
/ giving feedback on each drawing as if they all were the best things
/ they'd ever seen / pointing & suggesting / what they think would
be extra cool if i tried it / i liked them immediately / liked that they,
too, were "them" immediately but didn't assume i knew what kind of
"them" just because we're alike / "from the same team" / already living
somewhere far / past the binary at age twelve escaping hell in our
imaginary worlds suddenly feeling like / with this new friend / what's
inside my head

could become real

after school that day i showed them

everything i'd collected in the room my folks used to sleep in

> how i'd turned the space into a studio & their bed frame into a
> desk

past the security guards pretending to watch over our projects

> we crossed the courtyard to my building before the streetlights
> came on

took the elevator up to the fifth floor where the doors shook
themselves open

> after school that day i showed them how i'd learned

to create what i'd never seen while my big sister gave me all the
secondhand

> warnings she could remember from before we were on our
> own

passed down to keep us in check out of fear that breaking rules

> would cost us our freedom

too

IRV

i never cut nobody like Cerulean's hair until my sib Jai told me
& Cerulean to meet them at their house one Saturday. it wasn't
no different than any other Saturday back then cause that's what
me & Jai always did. i would bring chocolate milk & Jai would let
me cut their hair any way i wanted. first we'd eat big-ass blueberry
pancakes—the kind you make when ain't no adults around to tell you
it's too much sugar—while watching barber how-to videos. then Jai
would sketch a mood or a feeling they wanted & then let me figure
out the cut. only difference that Saturday was Cerulean. i didn't know
they was coming & that they would be my first real customer.

Cerulean didn't know either. it was weird though. they didn't seem
mad. or nervous at the idea of somebody their age cutting their hair.
they just dapped me up & told me "take off the back" as they dropped
down onto the stool Jai had set up in the middle of the bathroom.

i'm not gon' lie: i was scared. we were fifteen & i wasn't sure about this
barber shit. truth was i just needed my own way to make more money
so i could get me a computer. so i could eat. so i could survive. but Jai
didn't know all that. nobody did.

anyway—they had a whole head of dreads, telling me to shave part
of their head. then Jai said Cerulean was gonna pay me ten dollars.
i found a picture on Instagram that i thought looked cool & easy
enough & showed it to them so i knew it would be okay. it was called
an undercut & Cerulean just smiled back at me like it was the best day
ever. after a few minutes they added, *plus i used to be bald when i was a*
baby so i could do that again if anything happens.

i could be free again. just like a lil baby.

it only took a few minutes to cover Jai's bathroom floor with Cerulean's locs

the rest of their hair
tied in a knot
at the top of their head
Cerulean's skin looked
baby-like under
the old sepia sink light
bare & perfect

but i couldn't
stop my hand
from shaking
as i moved
the clippers closer
to where i wanted

to

make

a

clean

line

between

the

part

they

didn't

want anymore

& everything

they

wanted

to

keep

you hesitating like you scared, fam

you think i don't
know what i'm asking for

that's why you're
so nervous

you don't believe
i know

what i want
but i do

haven't you
done this

hella times
before?

before Cerulean

before Jai

it was just
me & my clippers
me & my pens
me & my notebooks
me & the 6 train
me & my beliefs
that ima be
tryna survive
alone
forever

it's easy to make friends

meet all types
of people
who are curious
about you
want to know
your name
get into all
kinds of shit
while it still
being harder
to keep anyone
around
when you've
always
got a secret
something
you rather
people not
know
something
you rather
people not
worry about
at risk
of them looking
at you
like some type
of charity case

it's easy
to make friends
even harder
to claim a family
trying to hide
where you live
or more so where you don't / can't
hardest
to form bonds
when your bed
is the train
between two & six
a.m.

you ever heard the mythology of the 6 train

is how i tried to change the subject / that night we rode the 6 train /
"home" together / Cerulean took the bait / ain't make a big deal at me /
ignoring / their questions about / my stop my neighborhood my block
my family as we got closer to theirs / they said they'd never heard / of
anything like it / i told them / there's a story / an urban legend about
the closed subway stations all over the city / that people who've found /
a way to get off on one of those stops / always seemed to go missing

you not worried about missing your stop? Cerulean asked

nah . . . so anyway like i was saying
people get off at these stops right
but don't nobody really know where
they are   or what they lead to
they just get off & nobody
ever sees them again   or at least
they don't see them for a very long time

oh yeah?
that sounds kind of nice
they pause lookin like
they thinkin a little too deep
about what i just said
& how . . . do these people find
the stop?

easy   a lot of those folks
find it by never getting off
at the Brooklyn Bridge stop
i tell them while wondering why
they wanna know
when you get to that stop   on the 6
you just hide so don't no cops
try to stop you from stayin on

Cerulean thinks harder
as if they're making
weird calculations in their mind

then shakes their head
waving off whatever had bounced
around in their mind for those few minutes
like a fly that ain't supposed to be here
but somehow still is

the train wheels screech to a loud halt at Cerulean's stop

they look over at me
to shake my hand
say goodbye

they don't bother
to ask me why i'm
staying on

they never ask me
where i'm going
they just

seem to know
when to offer me
a coat   a blanket   a plate of their father's food

silence

III.

AIRYN

Iya says Cerulean was first to hold me after she pushed me out.
says Baba fainted in the corner across the room and that she was too
scared to touch the person who'd almost killed her being born. too
much blood lost to face me. to look at the person who'd caused her all
that pain. so the doctor handed me to the only other person who was
there. it didn't matter that Cerulean was only ten years old at the time.
somehow   they were the only one who seemed ready. Iya says
Cerulean was reading aloud to me when she finally woke up from her
after-birth nap. & that i was staringstaringstaring into their eyes from
the incubator next to Iya's hospital bed.

Cerulean said they remember things different. that it was Cerulean
that couldn't face me. said that, even back then, it was hard to feel
happy about me being born into the chaos of this world. said they only
held me cause there was no other family in the room and wasn't no
way they could let the doctors wrap me up and tuck me somewhere
without me touching somebody familiar. somebody safe. truth is they
never believed i could be safe outside Iya's belly. truth is Cerulean
wished i could have remained a safe spirit that lived somewhere up
in the sky where this world couldn't reach me. Iya says they cried and
cried until she reminded them that they get to give me both my names.

soon as i was old enough to walk me and Cerulean were outside.
& soon as i could talk they taught me their favorite game called
imagine where Cerulean would point to things we saw on the block
and imagine it being used for something different. i would point to
everything from birds to trash to cops to blue mailboxes on the corner
and Cerulean would make up a story about whatever it was on the
spot. last time we played that game was in our backyard like a month
before Baba got hurt.

if i'd known what was gon' happen, i would have asked to play our game one more time. i would have asked to play *imagine* in our garden. i would have asked Cerulean to help me imagine this house without them instead of being sad that my flowers might die.

you keep sayin "come back"

like what you mean ain't that they're gonna die
i'm old enough to know they just gonna die, Cerulean

—not true, Bubby, the name only i call him
i learned about plants & shit, too, you know

they're not that different from the stuff i'm tryna grow.

not true, Bubby

they're not that different from the stuff i'm tryna grow.

Bubby

somehow   outside

things   look   dead

but [they've only] gone back

to   the soil

about a week before Cerulean disappeared the kitchen stunk
of Baba's sourdough cinnamon bread. that's what they said i should
make for the family because *every*body loves bread & with Baba
being on bed rest, it would be perfect timing. they made me run back
& forth all over the kitchen searching for sugar, butter, flour, eggs,
measuring cups, spoons, the scale, until sweat drizzled from every
part of my body. then they made me set it all up carefully, telling me
to remember that baking is chemistry & that i'd ruin it if i tried to
skip the math. i rolled my eyes, reminding them it was a half day &
school was out. no speeches. still i wanted to get it right &, most of
all, i wanted Cerulean to be proud of me.

once every tool & ingredient was set up they told me how to use Baba's
starter. told me some people call it a mother. when my face scrunched
at this they held up their hands & told me to relax. we don't have to
start all the way from scratch.

already in this house one has existed and it's still. alive.

to keep a starter alive, all you need is flour, water & a big glass jar. told me if there were bubbles, that means it is alive. it is already successful. told me if it is alive & strong it won't sink when i drop a piece in water. told me that as long as i keep an eye on it, keep feeding it with flour, water & air, it could take care of me forever.

a week later, Cerulean was gone.

at first Iya didn't believe me when i told her i knew Cerulean was still alive. Baba didn't either. days of searching turned to weeks. weeks turned to months. nobody slept & i was excused from school for the first month. we all grieved & then we were back . . . to normal. i waited a whole year. & i'd known for a year before that. it doesn't matter that they don't call. it doesn't matter that they didn't leave a note. it doesn't matter that they didn't tell anybody when they left in the middle of the night. it was obvious that it wasn't by force. their bike was gone. they'd left the cargo pants & graphic tees they said would one day fit me. they'd left the sneakers they said i could one day sell to help save money for my own farm. they'd left me another mother.

but for the first year that Cerulean was gone, we stayed out of our kitchen mostly. it grew thick mold crusts & sour smells that reeked so bad that it became what kept us from dealing with it. until Baba's hands started working the way he needed them to again. after all the physical therapy had brought back his fingers' functions & there was full feeling in the nerves, Baba started his dream all over again.

that's when he started poking at me about mine.

birthdays became weird around here for a long time after everybody accepted that they were never coming back. it's been about ten years since i last saw my big sib & after months of Iya & Baba asking me what i want for turning seventeen i knew exactly how to spend it & what to do.

Baba turns out the lights in the living room

while Iya sets up the projector
she first bought for their room
when Baba's cooking limbs
were still
useless

from behind all the jars of pickles
packages of cheese
plastic containers of leftovers
i dig out the mother
Cerulean left me

the one Baba had forgotten

from the back of the fridge
put it on the counter seeing it
look just as alive as the day
i found it not wanting to touch it

at first

THIS WEEK ON DYSTOPIA TANK RACE

TEN COMPETITORS
SET OUT
FOR THE BIGGEST
OPPORTUNITY
OF A LIFETIME

in just over an hour
the whole house will
smell like bread

TEN YOUNG TRAVELERS
FROM ALL
ACROSS AMERICA
COMPETE FOR TWO HUNDRED
THOUSAND DOLLARS
TO START THEIR OWN   COMMUNITIES

we're making
two loaves:
one for now
the other for a three-day
cross-country trip ahead

TONIGHT WE MEET
TEN YOUNG TRAVELERS
ON THE FIRST-EVER
WEST COAST
SEASON & FIND OUT

the one tonight will have
coconut & flecks of lavender i grew
right in our backyard
sprinkled on top

WHO HAS WHAT IT TAKES
TO LIGHT OUT FOR THE TERRITORY

Iya does what she always does

when we watch anything loosely together:
starts flipping through show trailers
if she thinks me or Baba
aren't paying enough attention

i see her get trapped by a Hulu commercial
for a new iPhone update
that can tell parents pretty much
anything their child wouldn't

want them to know
                Cerulean isn't a child anymore
& i can hack into any
computer system i touch

i see the family on the projection
smile feeling relief to learn
their kid is just down the street
their kid has eaten twice today

their kid skipped class at 11:42
their kid texted their best friend an hour ago
their kid seems to come back safe
their kid looks like their home

is somewhere they wanted
to come back to
                Cerulean doesn't want to come back

& the commercial kid still lives in an unchanged
        America

i try

& tune out the background noise
of Iya's continued channel flipping
while i decide to check out the news
aka a quick scroll through

Snapchat
Instagram
TikTok
YouTube

Baba announces it's almost
time to examine our first
loaf of sweet sourdough
poked seventeen times by birthday candles

a new tradition we started
just a few years ago
decorating ordinary foods
to celebrate the fact that

we're still here even
when life ain't so sweet
all the time & at any second
we could lose contact

with somebody we love

all seventeen candles taunt me

so i focus my eyes back
on my phone's screen
notice everyone resharing
a picture of another teenager

missing

my heart races at the thought
of that once being Cerulean
my heart drops remembering
that now it couldn't be

it's been ten years
& everyone knows
amber alerts that last
that long

are reserved for white girls
but i know

Cerulean isn't missing

Iya finally settles back on *Dystopia Tank Race*

unable to find anything else more entertaining
or exciting enough to play in the background
of my small little birthday party
places the remote down
& wanders over to the kitchen
to clear the counter
picking up a pile of envelopes
at the end of the counter needing
to be put away

since when do people mail things
without return addresses? she asks
skimming through them one by one
she notices Baba & me staring her
up & down for getting distracted
by Adulting shit on my birthday
& stuffs the colorful stack of envelopes
in the junk drawer where i'll
steal them from later
before getting on the road

Baba points to the projection and says

ain't none of them gon' survive much
without being able to make one of these

he gestures at the warm loaf
looking at it like it's the key to life

to survive you need to feel powerful
& you can't feel that if you don't

know how to make something
out of almost nothing

i try to tune out Baba's voice
when he starts sounding

like he's about to deliver
a sermon or lecture

tell me what's more powerful
than knowing how to feed yourself?

tell me what's more powerful
than creating your own source?

& focus my eyes on the show
until he calls me by my name

Airyn, he says

i know you getting grown now

& your mind probably going
all kinds of places

your mama & i
ain't gonna stop you

Baba lights the candles
& tells me to make a wish

Cerulean isn't found
Cerulean isn't lost

Acknowledgments

I first began writing *Salt the Water* for fun. This book was born of my desire to play again: to shake things up in way a that felt irreverent, defiant, honest, exciting, and about something much bigger than me. I wanted to go back to before I began fearing consequence or whether my art could feed me. I wanted to love it the way I first did as a sophomore at Howard University showing up at open mics every week, hungry to be moved and in deep connection. What this journey became was nothing of what I originally expected. Like many in this new world of too much noise, I also had forgotten what brevity, line break, and breath can do. What writing in verse can do for a story that is trying to take shape, having been unsuccessful at being heard any other way.

My gratitude is endless for those who have never once tried to urge me backward: literary community, extended family, mentors, friends, and supporters who have encouraged me to look deeper into all the dark places and honor them for what they are. Thank you for pushing me closer to myself, thusly pushing me further away from the things that cannot accept me and mine whole. Thank you for calling me by my name so I can call us all by our names.

What I mean to say is this: to watch our world shift in ways that could truly make many of us fear for our lives just for being ourselves, thank you, Dear Reader, Dear Family, Dear Loved One, for protecting us (because this is how you truly love us). Thank you for fighting for our right to tell stories of full, blossoming human beings. Beings who deserve to exist both in real life, in books, in the future, & & & . . .

There were many who made this novel come to fruition without knowing it. There were a handful who did so intentionally, holding my hand throughout various shots in the dark and experiments. Thank you to my readers and listeners when this book was still in its infancy. You know who you are. Thank you to every loved one who offered a couch, a listening ear, a meal, a safe shoulder to cry into during all the many unglamourous parts of being an author and person. Thank you to a whole community of folk who provided the conditions and resources to help me finish writing this story during one of hardest summers of my life.

This book doesn't end the way one might expect it to because of all of you. Because of you, I continue to use fiction to imagine something different. All of you give me continued hope in goodness, imagination, creativity, and love. You all inspire me to remember that in all I do and all I write, I must truly live.